The
TREK

Sean Kikkert

This book is dedicated to my parents,
who sacrificed so much for me,
and who have always been there for me.

ACKNOWLEDGMENTS

As my first published book, The Trek has a special place in my heart, and I will always remember those who have helped me, encouraged me and stood by me throughout this labour of love.

Firstly, I wish to thank my Heavenly Father. I believe that I am dependent on God for everything and that all good things come from Him. I am a witness of His love for His children, and it is my hope that, at least in a small way, I have been able to reflect His love through my words.

I gratefully acknowledge Sylvia Wang for all her dedication, generosity and support in designing the cover for this book.

I thank my friend, my brother and my editor, Dr Brett Charles Baker, for always being there for me and always making time for me.

I am grateful to Linda Prince for her comments on my manuscript. Linda's kindness and generosity in reading my manuscript and providing me with feedback has made me a better writer.

I thank my photographer, Jeremy Mann, for his generosity, dedication and artistic vision. I am also grateful to

Eden Sellick, Jose Alvarado and Evan Harvey for their help and support.

I gratefully acknowledge Erin McPhee for modelling Chelsea for the book cover, as well as Victoria's Models for helping me find the perfect model for my cover.

I thank Boyd Tuttle and Digital Legend Press for giving me this opportunity to see my first book published.

Lastly, I thank my wife Elizabeth and my children for their patience while I wrote this book. My book and my life have been enriched by true friends and family who have influenced me for good, and they all have my deep gratitude.

PREFACE

The idea for writing The Trek first came to me as I helped push a handcart across the rugged terrain of the Australian bush. I was then serving as the stake young men president and had volunteered to attend our stake's pioneer trek re-enactment in a support role. But when I saw a group of youth who were struggling with their handcart, I knew I had to join this "family" and lend them a hand. No doubt many members of handcart companies in the nineteenth century did the same thing.

As I participated, I saw the impact that trek was having on our youth, and I witnessed how much they grew when they were tested physically, mentally, spiritually and emotionally. I loved the blend of adventure, monotonous hard work, spirituality and raw emotions that characterised each day.

As a convert, I had missed out on many of the adventures that youth in the Church frequently enjoy, but I have been blessed to share in some of those experiences as an adult leader. I am also grateful for the opportunity I had to serve for several years in the Australian Army Reserve, and especially for the time spent out bush. Like Chelsea in the story, I have found some of these experiences difficult—from sleeping on cold ground to leaving my old life behind—but I have grown from them, too.

Youth and adults facing challenges together in a wilderness setting seemed to have all the ingredients for a great story. As I pushed together with my trek family, I could see the suspense-thriller that you are about to read unfolding in my mind. I hope you enjoy reading it as much as I enjoyed writing it!

CHAPTER 1

I beamed with satisfaction as I gazed at my reflection in the mirror. The girl that stared back at me looked pure and clean and even radiant. My nineteenth-century dress gave me an aura of innocence; one that was at odds with the worldly and shadowy life that I had lived up until six months ago. Seeing this simple, wholesome life reflected back at me through the mirror, I realised how much I longed for this goodness.

I wasn't looking forward to roughing it, despite my commitment to becoming the pure, innocent-looking girl that I saw reflected back at me from the mirror. In fact I dreaded the thought of pushing a handcart until my hands and feet blistered; of sleeping on the cold, hard ground each night; and especially of going four days without a shower. But if doing this would enable me to develop the pure, simple faith of a pioneer, I was willing to make that sacrifice.

While I had never looked more virtuous and more innocent, I knew that my clean and wholesome beauty wouldn't last. I would be a mess after four days of pushing a handcart over the dusty Australian countryside. I scrunched up my nose in disgust as I thought about how I would smell after four days without a shower. I had never gone that long in my life without my creature comforts. I was a city girl through and through, and I had lived my whole life in comfort with little experience in going without.

A knock at my bedroom door shook me back to the present. Dad stepped into my small, functional bedroom and leaned against the wardrobe. My wardrobe was much smaller than what I had been used to, and it appeared tiny next to my Dad's enormous frame. In another life I had enjoyed an enormous room crammed with everything that a teenage girl could want. My current room felt so sterile and lifeless in comparison, and I knew that I would never be that well off again.

"Ready to go, Chelsea?" Dad asked, motioning to me with a nod of his head. I suppressed a laugh when I looked at what Dad was wearing. Dad was an extremely large man with huge shoulders and a massive chest. He always seemed to see everything, and most people were naturally intimidated by him. And they had good reason to be if they knew his background. But that didn't square off with Dad's costume. Although Dad had gone for the humble farm boy look, he had failed miserably. Even in his suspenders, chequered shirt and straw hat, Dad still looked like a thug.

"You still look more like a gangster than a pioneer," I quipped. I had only meant it as a smart comment, one of those dumb things you say without thinking. Dad, however, took it earnestly. "Well, my heart has changed," he told me as he stroked his chin, "but it probably takes a bit longer for the outside appearance to catch up. Who knows, maybe I'll always look like a gangster. But that's not who I am any more, Chelsea."

What Dad had said was true. While he still looked and acted scary, and had certain mannerisms that would probably be with him for life. I never knew someone could change so much in such a short period of time, and having Dad come on trek with me was a miracle really. All the same, I wasn't overjoyed that Mum and Dad were coming on trek as a Ma and Pa. Up until recently, I had feared more than loved Dad. Although I respected him, we had never been close. I consoled myself with the assurance that at least they wouldn't be my Ma and Pa. I knew that they always split family members on trek.

I glanced at my watch and saw that it really was time to get moving. "Okay, I'm ready," I said as I grabbed my sleeping bag and rucksack. And with that we were on our way.

"C'mon, Chelsea, time to wake up!" Dad called out to me. I opened my eyes and tried to turn my neck to look out of the window, but it hurt. It had been such a long drive, and I had spent most of it napping in the back of the car.

I knew that I wouldn't be getting much sleep over the next four days, so I figured I might as well rest while I could.

Rubbing my still sore neck, I gazed out of our dusty windows and saw that we had parked in front of this magnificent old Catholic church with crooked stone walls and a steeple that spiralled high into the sky. Gravestones were dotted sporadically throughout the churchyard, and the church was surrounded by high oak trees. Scattered around the church was a sea of youth in bonnets and broad-rimmed hats. I approached the church and traced the exterior with my hand. I love old buildings, and this church was truly beautiful. Touching it gave me the same feeling I got when I visited the Spoleto Cathedral during a family holiday in Italy. Although this old church was only a dwarf in comparison, I still got that same feeling of being part of something bigger and older than myself.

I breathed in the country air and savoured the fresh feel in my lungs. Looking at my watch, I saw that we still had half an hour to go before trek would begin. Wandering around the churchyard, I was surprised to see that many of the graves were much more recent than I had expected. Although the church must have been over a hundred years old, some of the graves were less than a decade old.

Blocking the sun with my hand, I squinted at the road ahead. It was so rugged and hilly. Most of the youth were chatting among themselves, and I searched the crowd for familiar faces. I found Bridget chatting with two other girls from my ward and made my way towards them. Bridget's eyes danced as she saw me approach, and she gave me a big grin. Reassurance flooded through me now that I was with my best friend. Bridget was a beautiful girl of seventeen with blond, curly hair and vivid blue eyes. "I just hope that it doesn't rain," Bridget whined to her other friends as she eyed the dark clouds overhead. "I know that the pioneers pushed their handcarts through snowstorms," she continued as I sat down next to her, "but I don't want to get all wet and miserable."

"Rain won't be the problem," a girl I knew as Marcia replied matter-of-factly as she tossed her curly brown hair out of her eyes. "It's the heat that I'm worried about. Did you know that it's going to be over ninety-five degrees all week long?"

I groaned just thinking about the suffocating heat. Bridget was just about to say something further when the eerie call of the bugle filled the air. "Can I have everyone's attention!" a grey-haired man with a thick neck and huge, muscular arms roared. Despite being so tough looking, his manner was relaxed and friendly. This was Mark Wilder, our trail boss, and all the youth obediently stopped in mid-conversation to listen to him. Everyone was eager to find out what family they had been assigned to.

I was relieved, but not surprised, when Brother Wilder announced that Bridget and I would be in the same family. My pulse raced as I waited for my Ma and Pa to be announced. My anticipation, however, quickly turned to horror as Brother Wilder read the names. "No, it can't be!" I gasped.

CHAPTER 2

"No!" I shrieked again, and all the youth near me turned and stared at me. I looked down with embarrassment. I hadn't wanted to draw attention to myself, and I felt very self-conscious among all these youth that I didn't know. With a sinking heart, I stepped towards my Ma and Pa. Dad looked over and gave me a wink, but I lowered my head to avoid his gaze. I was angry and felt betrayed. I knew that it wasn't Mum and Dad's fault, but at that moment I really resented being placed in their family. So much for keeping families separated, I thought bitterly. I shot Bridget a look of disgust. She gave me a sympathetic smile and just shrugged her shoulders.

This wasn't how it was meant to go, I fumed. How could this have happened? With resignation, I walked over to meet the rest of my family. There was nothing that could be done now, so I might as well make the best of it that I could.

While I didn't know any of the other youth in the family, I couldn't believe my luck when I saw the "older brother" of the family. He was an extremely handsome eighteen year old with broad shoulders and a dazzling smile. "My name is Peter," he told the group as he raised his hand in a casual wave. I knew straightaway that Peter would be a good member of the family. Not only was he good looking, but he was tall and muscular and looked like he could push the handcart all by himself.

I realised that we would be relying on Peter's brawn when I saw the rest of the family. As well as Bridget and me, there was a puny fourteen-year-old boy named Steve with thick dark hair, dramatic brown eyes and a serious expression, and a delicate-looking seventeen-year-old girl named Carly with long brown hair, high cheekbones and piercing green eyes. Steve looked too scrawny to be much help in pushing the handcart, and Carly, like me, looked like she wasn't particularly used to roughing it.

"Attention, everyone," Dad demanded after everyone had introduced themselves. "We are going to have a shakedown." Our family just stared at Dad blankly and it was clear that no one had any idea what he was talking about.

"That means I'm going to search you for phones, electronics, food, or any other banned items," Dad explained, and his expression suddenly turned deadly serious. "Make no mistake," he growled. "I have plenty of experience searching people for hidden objects. If you have it, I'll find it."

A look of horror flashed over Carly's face. I wondered what she had hidden and where. Looking at the group, I noticed that all of the kids were looking pretty worried. "Stop it!" Mum whispered fiercely in Dad's ear. "You're scaring them." Mum then turned to us. "We trust you," she told us sweetly. "If you have anything you shouldn't have, just tell us now. We're not going to search you."

I rolled my eyes. They were playing good cop/bad cop. They'd used the same routine on me countless times in order to get a confession. This was exactly why I should have a different Ma and Pa for Trek. I already knew all their tricks.

Peter and Steve were struggling to tie down our belongings to the handcart when I saw Keith Lawson, our company captain, making his way towards Dad. Brother Lawson was a tall, thin man with glasses and a bald spot on the back of his head. Dad turned to greet him, but Dad's smile quickly faded when he saw Brother Lawson's long, determined strut and the cold, mean expression on his face. Brother Lawson clearly had a bone to pick with Dad.

Brother Lawson ignored Dad's outstretched hand as he approached us. "I can't believe that they made you and your wife a Ma and Pa," he spat at Dad bitterly. "You haven't even been a member of the Church for six months. You can't possibly have the gospel maturity for an important role like that!"

Dad always remained calm when confronted, and I always admired how he never let his anger show. Although he must have been seething inside, he spoke in a calm, controlled manner, and there wasn't even a hint of annoyance in his voice. "Many of the pioneers were new converts too," he pointed out evenly. "Regardless of whether we have pioneers for our ancestors or whether we were baptised a week ago, if we have a desire to serve God, we are called to the work."

Brother Lawson gave a cruel, hard laugh. "You may think that you have everyone fooled," he snorted, "but not me". Brother Lawson's eyes dimmed. "I know you have a dark past. I objected to you being called as a Pa, but President Strong insisted. But I know you don't belong here!"

Dad's face remained inexpressive, but I could read Dad better than most. And I saw the flash of anger and hurt in his eyes. But Dad did not respond. Instead he turned his back on Brother Lawson and continued tying down the handcart. I really hoped that Brother Lawson would take the hint and not provoke Dad, but Brother Lawson seemed reluctant to back off. He looked like he had more to get of his chest, and so he just stood there awkwardly for a moment. After what seemed like an eternity, Brother Lawson stormed off, and I let out a breath of relief and immediately relaxed. "What was that all about?" I whispered to Dad once Brother Lawson was out of earshot. Dad just shrugged. "Who knows, Chelsea," he sighed. "Maybe he does know something about our past. It's clear that he doesn't want us here. It's a good thing that it's not up to him."

I was angry at the way that Brother Lawson had spoken to Dad. It really bothered me. A knot began to form in the pit of my stomach, and I suddenly felt very uncomfortable. Self-consciousness swept over me, and I wondered how many other people felt the same way. Were there others who thought that we didn't belong? If so, I was determined to prove them wrong.

Dad looked over at our handcart and sighed. It was a lopsided, tangled mess, nothing at all like the perfect bundle that the Semmler family had created. Their handcart was so well-ordered, I wondered if someone in their family had obsessive-compulsive disorder. Brother Semmler looked over and saw us all staring at his handcart. "It's my army training," he explained sheepishly. "We are taught that everything has its place, and to order things so we can find it when we need it."

We turned away from Brother Semmler's handcart and stared again at the chaos that was our own handcart. Dad gave a big sigh. "Time to fix up this mess so we can get on the road," Dad ordered in a loud, bellowing voice. "You'll find that the handcart will be much easier to push if we can just balance it out properly."

Once each family's handcart was loaded, President Strong, our stake president, stepped forward. He was wearing a cravat and had a long, straggly beard plastered to his face. "Brothers and sisters," President Strong bellowed, using in his best Brigham Young impersonation, "we have been persecuted wherever we have gone. All of you have suffered so much. But God has prepared a place for us where we can build His Kingdom without oppression. Mobs will never force you from your homes again. There is a place for us where we will live out our days in peace." President Strong paused and pointed towards the hills that twisted ahead. They continued for as far as the eye could see, and I felt exhausted at the very thought of pushing a handcart over them. "You must go to Zion!" President Strong roared at us like a lion. "To Zion!" we all yelled back in unison, and I felt electrified as I joined in the chorus. For the first time in my life, I felt a sense of unity with others my age.

It really did feel as if Heavenly Father had entrusted us all with a godly task.

And with that we were off. Peter, Bridget and I began pushing from the front, and Carly and Steve pushed from behind. At first, pushing the handcart didn't seem so bad. I had expected it to be much harder. However, I changed my mind once the path began to slope uphill. The neck of my pretty purple dress quickly turned dark with sweat, and the muscles in my shoulders began to knot up. As the hours dragged on, the path just became steeper and steeper. I focused on taking one step after another and tried to ignore the dull ache in my neck and back. I shot a quick look at Peter and saw that his face was tightly knitted in concentration. He saw me look over and flashed a smile back at me, and my heart skipped a beat.

Soon the path began to slope downwards, and I discovered that that was even harder. I was now using a whole different set of muscles to hold the handcart back against gravity. I was so relieved when the handcart in front of us stopped, forcing us to also halt. I poured warm water from my water bottle all over my head and inhaled deep mouthfuls of air before we resumed pushing.

Eventually we arrived at a beautiful, flowing river. We dropped the handcart, and I stretched my aching back. At first I just enjoyed the tranquil scene. The sound of flowing waters made me feel peaceful and calm. I savoured the strong, cool wind that blew against me. However, a knot began to form in the pit of my stomach when I suddenly realised that we were going to have to cross the river.

Bridget began to massage my tight shoulders. "How are you doing, Chelsea?" she asked me kindly. "Okay so far," I sighed, "but they're not really planning on making us cross that river, are they?" Bridget and I both just stood there staring at the river, and Bridget and I then exchanged worried glances. I had heard rumours that there might be a water-crossing on trek, but I hadn't expected anything like this.

Dad called the family in. "Sorry, everyone, we had expected there to be just a stream here," Dad apologised. "It's been raining a lot lately, and so there's much more water than we expected. However, we can all cross safely as long as we are careful and all work together. Ma and I will carry the handcart across the river. I want everyone else to help each other across. Peter, why don't you be a gentleman and carry the girls across the river?"

Peter nodded, and I felt a wave of excitement at the thought of Peter scooping me up in his strong, powerful arms and carrying me safely across the river. I knew that I would feel so safe, so secure in his arms. My heart dropped, however, when Steve unexpectedly piped up. "I can carry someone too!" he insisted. "How about I carry Chelsea?"

Dad hesitated for a moment. He seemed a little uncertain, but then Dad nodded, and with that Mum and Dad began their struggle to push the handcart across the river. I saw that Peter had already scooped up Bridget and was halfway across the river with her, and I envied her. Bridget was beaming happily in Peter's arms, and I saw her laugh heartily in response to something that Peter said. I looked Steve up and down again but didn't feel encouraged by what I saw. Steve was already looking haggard and worn out from his journey, and he really didn't look strong enough to carry any of us girls across the river. "You don't need to carry me," I told him. "I can just walk across. I don't mind getting wet."

But Steve just shook his head. "No, let me carry you," he insisted. "It's my duty." I nodded and, placing my arm around Steve's shoulder, stepped into his arms. I was surprised at Steve's strength as he began to carry me. He was stronger than he looked, and his muscles felt hard and toned. It was such a hot day, and the water felt so nice and cool as it splashed up on me as Steve carried me across the river.

Once we reached the middle of the river, however, I could sense that Steve was beginning to fade. He continued to force his way forward, but all of a sudden his knees buckled, his legs gave way under him, and he dropped me into the water with a big splash. Before I could react, I was being swept under by the current. I fought against it with all my strength, but the current was just too strong and kept on forcing my head under the water. My head was beginning to spin now. I struggled to the surface and deeply inhaled a mouthful of air. And then I was under again. I forced myself to hold my breath, even though my lungs were screaming for air. There was no way that I wanted to inhale that filthy river water. I was beginning to get dizzy now. My lungs were burning and felt like they would burst any second. My vision began to cloud over, and darkness was overcoming me. I couldn't resist the impulse to inhale any longer. This is it, I thought, panic rushing through my body. This is how I'm going to die.

CHAPTER 3

This was the end. I was grateful that I at least had got to embrace the restored gospel before dying. I knew that death would not be the end of my spiritual journey. I had only begun to flower on earth, and now I would fully blossom in heaven. All the same, I was terrified to die, and I thrashed about with all my might trying desperately to save myself. The darkness was now overcoming me, and I felt like I had little choice but to give in to it. I had no strength to fight it any more.

Just as I abandoned myself to the darkness, I felt a set of strong, muscular arms pulling me out of the water. As I looked up, I found myself gazing at Peter's handsome face. Looking around, I saw that Dad was helping Steve out of the water a little further upstream. Completely soaked through, Steve looked smaller and scrawnier than ever. When Dad saw my half-drowned body in Peter's arms, he turned white. Dad rushed over frantically, making huge splashes as he bulldozed his way through the water. He whisked me out of Peter's arms and carried me to the shore. "Are you alright, Chelsea?" he asked, his voice shaky with concern. Still gasping and coughing, I nodded.

Steve rushed over to my side and looked down at me. "Sorry about that," he spluttered sheepishly, avoiding my gaze. Exhausted and half-drowned, I just lay in the long grass. The company gathered around me, their faces strained with worry.

I could hear everyone talking about me, and I hated it. It made me so uncomfortable being the object of everyone's concern. I got up and took my place at the front of the handcart, but Dad shook his head. "Chelsea, you take a break from pushing the handcart for a while," Dad ordered. I opened my mouth to protest, but Dad gave me the look. And I remembered that I didn't argue with my father. Ever. And so I began walking beside the handcart while my family pushed.

Still wet and feeling like a drowned rat, I was beginning to feel sorry for myself. It was only the first day, but the road seemed to go on forever, and I was shivering from being soaked through. I was secretly glad that Dad had insisted that I take a break from pushing.

"Cheer up, Chelsea," Bridget called out to me as she wiped the sweat from her forehead with the sleeve of her dress. "At least the river wasn't filled with huge chunks of ice like it was for the pioneers." I shot Bridget a deadly look, and she immediately shut up. Carly glared at me, frowned, and then looked away.

The sun began to dry out my clothes as I marched along in the blazing heat. And as I walked, I pondered about how different my life was now compared to a year ago. Back then, I had been living in the lap of luxury, and if someone had told me that in a year's time I would be engaged in a religious historical re-enactment in the middle of the bush, I would have thought that they were crazy.

I'm certain that neither Dad nor I would have given the missionaries the time of day had we been the ones that had greeted them that afternoon. Luckily Mum was the one who answered the door. Mum had always been more spiritual than Dad or I had ever been. She had a sense about people, and she had a feeling that these two young women on her doorstep were good and pure people. She later told us that they just seemed to radiate light. Mum felt in her heart that they had something that her family needed, and she was determined to make sure that they had a chance to share whatever they had.

I stopped short when I came down from my room and saw the sister missionaries sitting at our dining room table devouring Mum's spaghetti. These two girls were emptying their plates like they hadn't eaten for a week, and Mum was just sitting back, beaming at them. The two women seemed to understand that the sure way to win Mum's heart was to enjoy her food.

I cleared my throat, making my presence known. "Mum, what's going on?" I demanded. Mum ignored my tone and waved me down the stairs. "Chelsea, come meet these girls," she beckoned. I looked the sister missionaries over. They were both dressed neatly, almost professionally, and wore huge smiles on their faces. While their smiles made me suspicious at first, I relaxed a little once I decided that their smiles were real. There was no pretence and no deception about them. There was a certain glow about these girls; it was as if warmth and light and love were radiating from them.

"Does Dad know that they're here?" I asked Mum tentatively. I felt pretty confident that Dad wouldn't like this.

Mum ignored my question and poured the girls big glasses of grape juice. I fixed myself a plate of spaghetti and began to eat nervously, keeping an ear out in case Dad came home. The girls wanted to know all about Mum, and she was busy telling them about her childhood in Sicily, when suddenly I heard a car pull up in the driveway. My eyes darted towards the door as I heard footsteps approaching. I wondered if I should leave, but I figured it was now too late.

Dad walked into the house humming cheerfully, but his mood changed the instant he saw the sister missionaries sitting at his dining room table eating his wife's spaghetti. I saw Dad stiffen, and everyone in the room tensed up. The two girls stood up to acknowledge Dad, but he wouldn't even meet their gaze. Instead of taking his jacket off and slouching down in his favourite armchair, like he normally would after returning home, Dad simply turned his back and stormed out of the house, slamming the door behind him.

I figured that this would be the last time that I would see those girls, but I was wrong. Mum just acted as if nothing was wrong and continued to chat to the girls while they finished eating. Once they were done, Mum invited them to come back the following night to share their message. "Are you sure it will be okay with your husband?" Sister Lata asked timidly. "He didn't seem too happy with us being here." Mum just shrugged. "Don't worry about him," she told them sternly. "You're here to see me, not him."

Mum's defiance surprised me, and I really couldn't recall another time that Mum had challenged Dad in this way. At first Dad would make himself scarce every time the sister missionaries visited us. He would either shut himself in the den or make a beeline for the front door. Eventually, however, Dad began to tolerate the sister missionaries' presence. And when they came over, the sisters always took the time to chat with Dad. They ignored his gruffness and rudeness, and they slowly began to win Dad over with their kindness and charm. Eventually Dad began to let his guard down, and his attitude to the sister missionaries began to soften. All the same, you could have struck me down with a feather when, after a few months, Dad casually announced over dinner one night that he was going to join Mum in listening to the sister missionaries' message. Once Dad began listening to the sisters, it felt like the most natural thing in the world for me to also join in. And as I listened to their message, I could feel my life changing week by week. Those changes brought my family peace, but they also brought us danger. We found that there were those who would rather kill us than let us change our ways.

I felt so much better once the afternoon sun finally dried me out. It was encouraging to see the sun fade behind the horizon. It meant that the day was almost over, and that we would soon be able to get some rest. "I can't believe we're going to sleep under the stars tonight," I whispered to Bridget excitedly. "I've never done that before in my life."

There wasn't much conversation happening at the moment. Everyone was so enthusiastic when we first began trek. Now, however, everyone was downcast and lost in their own thoughts. The silence was really getting to me, so I tried to start a conversation. "So how are you finding trek so far?" I asked Peter.

"I'm really glad I'm here," Peter told me. "I actually found it really hard to make the decision to come on trek. We have a big rugby game this Saturday, and I'm missing out on training this week. What's more, my team thinks that I'll be too worn out from trek to play my best on Saturday. Everyone gave me a pretty hard time for going. They told me that I was letting the team down and that it would be my fault if we lost the game. But I don't want my life to revolve around rugby. And I definitely don't want to miss out on spiritual experiences because of rugby."

Carly wiped her forehead with the back of her hand. "Peter, you're so good at rugby," she told him. "Everyone admires you and wants to be like you. If I were you, I would put rugby first. After all, it's rugby that is making you somebody."

Peter shook his head angrily. "I don't want people to look at me and just see a rugby player," he replied irritably. "If people are going to respect me, I'd rather they respect me for my spirituality than my rugby."

Carly just shrugged her shoulders, and we continued to push in silence. It was soon time to stop for a rest, and Mum and Dad led us in a devotional as we made ourselves as comfortable as we could in the grass. I felt an incredible feeling of peace and warmth as we sang "Come, Come, Ye Saints" together. "On this trek we're just giving you a little taste of what they pioneers sacrificed," Mum explained. "Although our sacrifices are nothing compared to what they sacrificed, you will grow closer to God through this experience. And I hope that you will always be glad that you came on trek."

The sun was setting over the horizon as we set out again. The hills were draped in orange-red, and the view was breathtaking. Stars began to fill the sky as it got darker and darker. Soon a million stars dotted the night. I tilted my head back and admired the moon and stars as we pushed. It was beautiful. You don't see anything like that in the city.

Suddenly an explosion of light filled the horizon. Moments later another deafening explosion ripped through the air, and soon there were flashes of light all around us. Suddenly the night sky was filled with angry voices shouting abuse at us. "We don't want you here!" a deep bellowing voice roared at us from my left. "Where are you going to, Mormons?" another man shouted out from the darkness. His voice was close; he couldn't have been more than ten metres away.

Dark, ominous figures were now beginning to step out of the shadows. My eyes fixed on an enormous man with broad shoulders and a huge chest who stepped out from behind a bush ahead of us. His shaggy beard trailed almost down to his waist. "We don't like Mormons around here," he growled at no one in particular. "We don't like you stinking up our land with your crazy ideas."

The bearded man strutted around cockily, surveying our company. Then he looked over in my direction, and our eyes met. Adrenaline surged through my body as he began sprinting towards me. I tried to reassure myself that he was just acting out the part of being a mob member. He was only trying to scare me and didn't really want to hurt me.

But I was wrong. My eyes bulged in horror as the man took an enormous leap straight at me. He flew through the air as if in slow motion. And then he crashed into me with a sickening thud.

My head exploded in pain as it bounced against the handcart. I tried to pull myself up from the ground, but my legs felt weak. A wave of dizziness swept over me, and my surroundings began swimming. I was trying very hard not to black out. I slowly pulled myself up and swayed on my feet, still gasping for the air that had been knocked from my lungs. My eyes focused on my attacker, and I saw that he was towering over me, ready to finish me off.

CHAPTER 4

I braced myself for the impending attack. My eyes searched my surroundings for anything that I could use to defend myself. It was so hard to think clearly. I was both dazed and frozen with fear. But I knew that I had to do something to defend myself against this much larger man. I scrambled and scooped up a large rock just as Peter pushed his way between us and gave my attacker a hard shove out of the way. The man was so large that the push barely moved him it all. "What on earth are you doing?" Peter demanded protectively, his hands balled into fists and the muscles in his neck tensed.

I waited for the man to lunge at Peter, but instead he began apologising profusely. "I really didn't mean to knock you over," he blurted to me. "It was so dark that I didn't see that log over there." The man gestured towards a large, decomposing log a few metres away. "I tripped over it while running, and it sent me flying through the air. I'm really sorry if I hurt you."

"Hurt her?" Peter retorted angrily. "You almost knocked her out. You could have seriously injured her."

"Peter, it's all right," I said, giving his shoulder a gentle squeeze. "No harm's been done. It was just an accident." The bloke apologised one final time before falling back into character as a mob member. "We don't want you here!" he barked at the Semmler family in front of us, kicking dirt at their eldest son, who glared back at him.

Brother Lawson was now weaving his way between the handcarts. "Keep calm, everyone," he called out in a soothing, reassuring voice. "Don't do anything to provoke the mob."

Eventually the mob had enough of kicking dirt at us and pushing us around and disappeared into the darkness as quickly as they had appeared. As we once again continued our journey, I was now so tired that I thought that I would fall asleep pushing the handcart. The back of my head still throbbed with pain, and I was grateful that the camp was only a short distance further. We finally arrived close to midnight, and I was starving. Dad got a fire started while Mum helped us set up a shelter with the tarps. The broth that Mum and Dad cooked did very little to fill our emptiness, but I was just happy to get something into my stomach.

The temperature had plummeted with the descending of the sun, and I leaned in nice and close to the fire and savoured the warmth on my face and upper body. We wanted to keep the cold at bay for as long as we could. Eventually, however, Dad stopped throwing sticks on the fire and allowed the flames to slowly die down. "Everyone to bed," he ordered. "We have a big day ahead of us, and we'll all feel much better tomorrow if we get a decent night's sleep."

I brushed my teeth and rinsed my mouth out with water from my drinking bottle. I poured some water on my hands and washed away the grime on my face. I would so love to have a hot, steamy shower right now, but that was probably the best wash that I would be able to manage while on trek. I didn't have a change of clothes, but thankfully I did have a change of socks. It felt so nice to tug off my boots and change into a fresh pair of socks before crawling into my sleeping bag. Being under the stars really was amazing. For the first time in my life, all the sacrifices that I had made for the gospel's sake didn't really feel like a sacrifice at all. I realised that I didn't need any of the stuff that I had given up.

I thought about the first sacrifice that I had ever made for the gospel's sake. I remembered feeling an intense sadness as I brushed my cascading blond hair with one hand while holding my mobile phone in the other. I had just washed my hair, and it smelt great. My make-up was carefully done, and I was wearing the white dress that I knew my boyfriend Paul liked best. Around my neck I wore the gold chain that I loved, the one that Paul had given me. While I was looking my best, my heart was heavy. I would be saying goodbye to a lot of things that night, and while I knew that these choices were right, I still needed to mourn for my old life. There were gaps in my heart and soul that the gospel hadn't filed as yet.

"Are you going to be all right?" Sister Green asked me over the phone. I was feeling sick to the stomach at the thought of my upcoming date with Paul. The sisters had taught me about the law of chastity during our last lesson, and I knew that Paul didn't want to live by the same standards that I did. He expected things of me that I couldn't give him. If I did, then I couldn't be the person that I wanted to be. Maybe my heart really was changing.

"Yeah, I'm okay," I assured Sister Green. "I know that this is the right thing to do. It feels hard though. I sometimes wish doing what is right was easier."

"It's never easy," Sister Green admitted. "That's the beauty of it. Every time we do what is right, it stretches us and makes us stronger."

I hung up and glanced at the clock on the wall. Paul would be here any minute, and I didn't see any other option but to break up with him. I was going to miss Paul. Tall and broad shouldered, with deep brown eyes and thick, wavy hair, Paul was so good looking. He was always confident and sure of himself. His father was one of the leading figures in our crime family, and I had grown up with Paul my whole life. Dad was very picky about who could take me out and insisted that my dates understood our way of life. Paul was one of the few boys that I had dated that Dad had actually approved of.

And Paul was smooth. He knew what to say to put everyone at ease and had a way of persuading people to do what he wanted. Most men in the mafia were smooth talkers, and of course I knew that they also had more sinister ways to convince people to do what they wanted. Underneath his charming exterior, I knew that Paul had a dark side. It was part of the life of all the men in the mafia, including my father.

The roar of the engine from the driveway announced that Paul had arrived in his shiny, black Porsche. I heard the clunk of the car door as Paul made his way to our doorstep. I remembered how impressed I had been the first time that Paul picked me up in that car. I had felt so luxurious, so sophisticated, like I was a movie star. People spend their whole lives working for money, power and prestige, and we had it all in our crime family. Paul and I were born into it. Now, however, as I casually glanced at the Porsche out of the window, I realised that all of the appeal had faded. I was no longer the kind of girl that could be impressed by being driven around in a fancy car.

Paul came to the door, and Dad gave him a big hug before Paul escorted me to the car. It was beginning to sprinkle, but Paul held an umbrella over me as he walked me to the passenger side and held the door open for me. That was one thing I loved about Paul. He was so well mannered, and he always treated me like I was a princess. And yet, underneath all that sophistication and thoughtfulness, there was a vicious side which I knew was not good for my life.

The Buckingham Arms was a favourite restaurant for our crime family, although plenty of ordinary people also dined there, completely oblivious to the shady deals being entered into a few tables across from them. The restaurant was well lit up with bright lights and wide glass windows, and it seemed so welcoming on such a wet, dark night. Paul slipped the usher a fifty dollar bill, and without a word the usher escorted us to a very secluded private table. Soon a waitress appeared to take our orders. Paul began to order wine for us, but I shook my head. "No, not for me," I explained. "I'll just have water." Paul frowned. "Okay," he conceded with a casual shrug, "water for both of us then."

The waitress returned a few minutes later with our orders. My steak looked amazing, and my mouth began to water just looking at it. I took a deep sniff and savoured the delicious aroma. I cut off a piece and bit into it. It was so tender and succulent, and the sauce was rich and creamy. The meat just melted in my mouth. Paul watched me smiling. He always took great pride in making sure I was happy with my meal.

Can I really do this? I wondered. I have such a good life, and I'm planning on just throwing it all away. And I wasn't just talking about riding in fancy cars and eating at pricey restaurants. I had been important my whole life because I was part of the Moretti crime family. Whenever I needed something, there was someone I could ask. We always had connections, and we always got special treatment. Did I really want to give it all up?

I was brought back to earth when I noticed that Paul was staring at me. "Okay, Chelsea, what's up?" he asked irritably. "You've been acting really strange." I gazed at a grey-haired couple on the other side of the restaurant. They looked like they were in their eighties, and yet they were gazing into each other's eyes as if they were on their first date. They must really love each other, I thought. As I watched them, I knew that that was what I wanted. I didn't want to be stuck with someone that I just liked being around. I wanted someone whom I could trust forever and who would be good for our future family. I wanted to build that family on goodness, grow old together, and eventually die knowing that we would be with each other in the eternities also. I knew Paul couldn't offer me any of this.

Seeing that I was still distracted, Paul decided to take a different approach. "Let's forget about talking," he said as he reached over and placed his hand over mine. "How about we go over to my place?" I looked up at him and saw that Paul had a suggestive grin plastered onto his face. However, Paul's wide grin quickly transformed into a frown as I shook my head. "Paul, I'm not the girl I used to be," I whispered solemnly.

Paul sighed. "Yeah, I can see that."

There was an awkward silence now, and so I figured that I might as well get this over and done with. "Look, Paul," I told him, "I think that we should break up. I think we're just on different paths now."

I'm not sure how I expected Paul to react, but I certainly didn't expect anything as violent as what followed. I jumped in alarm as Paul plummeted his enormous fist into the table. The table shook from the impact, and our glasses toppled over. I shrieked as icy water seeped from the table and onto the lap of my favourite dress. Thank goodness it was just water and not wine. It would be so embarrassing to walk out of the restaurant with a big red stain all over the lap of my beautiful white dress. I looked over and saw that the elderly couple across the room had stopped chatting and were now just staring at us.

Paul jumped to his feet angrily, his hands clenched into tight fists. Those deep brown eyes which had once seemed so warm and caring now glared at me coldly, and Paul's face turned bright red with rage. "You can't get rid of me that easily," Paul seethed through gritted teeth. He spoke with an angry, hard voice that I had never heard before. I met Paul's stare, refusing to look away. "I'll make you sorry," he promised, and his tone sent a chill up my spine. All the warmth had drained from him, I realised with a shudder of dread. He's really angry. What is he going to do to me?

CHAPTER 5

Paul's wave of anger seemed to pass as suddenly as it had begun. He now just stood on his feet awkwardly, his eyes darting around the restaurant. Paul's already red face turned even redder when he saw that everyone in the room was staring at him. He self-consciously slipped back into his seat and seemed to be just a withered, wounded husk of his former self. "I guess I'm holding you back, huh?" he said sadly with a faint smile. "I guess you've outgrown me."

There wasn't much to stay for after that, and so we quickly finished our meals, and I reluctantly got back into Paul's Porsche with him. With a soaked dress, I was no longer worried about getting wet in the rain on the way back to the car. Paul's angry outburst had scared me, and I kept a cautious eye on him as we rode in silence, the windscreen wipers swiping away the rain in wide arches. While Paul seemed much more subdued now, I didn't want to take any chances with him now that I had seen his nasty temper.

Paul pulled into the long driveway of our enormous, two-storey home. Our house looked dark and empty, which surprised me, as Mum and Dad were both at home when I left. I reached behind my neck and unhooked my gold chain. "What's this?" Paul asked with a sneer as I held the gold chain out for him.

"I'm giving you your gold chain back," I told him. "I know that it's expensive. You should give it to someone else."

Paul just shook his head. "Nah, keep it. Something to remember me by," Paul told me sadly.

I stepped out of the car. Without another word, Paul drove off furiously, his tires squealing, leaving me standing in the driveway. Paul normally didn't drive away until I was safely through the front door. I figured that he must be pretty upset with me.

The house was quiet as I walked through the front door. "Mum? . . . Dad? . . ." I called out, but there was no answer. They must have decided to go out after all. But I was wrong. As I flicked on the living room light, I saw that Mum and Dad were waiting for me with serious expressions on their faces. "Switch off the light!" Dad whispered fiercely. I obeyed. The only light that the room had was a dim glow from a single lamp. The room looked eerie; the dim light cast shadows everywhere. I saw that Dad was pacing the floor nervously. Dad was always so calm and in control, and so it was unsettling to see Dad so flustered.

"Dad, what's up?" I asked him, my voice edgy with concern.

CHAPTER 6

I shivered all night long on my first night of trek. Unable to sleep, I just lay there, my teeth chattering and my body curled into the foetal position against the cold. I listened to the wind howling through the trees and watched Peter snoring in his sleeping bag across the boys' side of our shelter. Peter looked so peaceful as he slept. He must have a pretty clear conscience, I thought. Unlike me. However it certainly wasn't my conscience that was keeping me up right now. I was sure that I would be able to fall right to sleep if I could just get a little warmer.

I felt like I had only just gotten to sleep when the bugle shook me from my slumber. Surely it can't be time to get up already! I thought with a groan. I really didn't want to get up and go through another day of this. I slowly opened my eyes. It was getting light outside, but only barely. The sky was still pretty dark. Although birds were beginning to chirp, I could sense that it was still very early.

I tried to close my eyes and fall back asleep, but Dad was soon shaking me. I tried to ignore him, but he just kept on shaking. "Were you planning on joining us, Chelsea?" he asked me sarcastically, "C'mon, the rest of the family are already up." I groaned again and pushed my tangled fringe out of my eyes. "What time is it?" I asked yawning.

"I don't know," he replied. "But it must be almost five o'clock."

"What!" I blurted. "You can't be serious, Dad. We only went to bed a few hours ago. Surely we can sleep a bit longer before we start."

"No, c'mon, Chelsea, it's time to go," Dad ordered. "This ain't no holiday camp."

The handcart felt heavy when we started pushing, much heavier than it had yesterday. I thought about how heavy the handcart must have felt to the pioneers who carried everything they owned over 1,300 miles through snow and ice. They were clearly much stronger than we are.

At first I tried to distract myself by chatting with the other members of my family. We were getting to know each other and were beginning to feel more comfortable in each other's presence. As the morning dragged on, however, our talk grew thinner as we became more and more tired.

Despite my exhaustion, I was really enjoying being out in nature. The sun wasn't too hot as yet and felt so nice on my face. I loved staring up at the clouds, listening to the chirping of the birds, and soaking up the magnificent views once we reached a peak. While I would gladly skip sleeping on the cold, hard ground, there was something very special about being out in nature. It made me feel alive in a way that I didn't usually. Being out in the bush had a calming, soothing affect on me.

As we pushed the handcart up a hill in the late morning, I noticed that there was a figure crouching in the distance. At first I thought it was some kind of animal. I blinked and looked again, but it was hard to see clearly because the sun was directly in my sight. As I focused my eyes, I realised that it was a young woman with long, straggly hair. As we approached her, I saw that she was covered in rags. "Drop the handcart," Dad ordered, but we had all already stopped.

I could tell that beneath her dirt-streaked face she was young and pretty. She must have been in her early twenties. Her eyes were amazing. They were dramatic and green, although they were now rimmed red from crying. I felt a chill run down my spine when I saw the tiny little bundle that she was clutching in her arms. The woman wiped tears from her eyes and stretched her hand out to us. "Please," she begged, "I'm so hungry. I need your help."

Dad reached into the handcart and pulled out a sandwich which he handed to the woman. She wolfed it down greedily with one hand while tightly clutching the tiny bundle to her chest with her other. "Are you okay?" Peter asked her kindly once she had finished eating.

"My child has died," the woman sobbed. "We were going to Zion as a family. But first my husband died. And then my child died. And now I'm all alone in the world."

"We'll help you bury your child," Peter told her tenderly. Without another word, Peter grabbed our shovel from the cart and began digging a hole at the side of the road. My heart went out to this woman. I so wanted to help, but each family only had one shovel between them. However, the older brothers from the other families saw what Peter was doing and began to join in one by one. Together they quickly dug a deep grave, and Peter reverently took the bundle from the woman's arms and placed it in the ground. "Is it okay if we sing a hymn together?" Mum asked our new friend, and she nodded sadly. Mum led us in singing "Come, Come, Ye Saints." Once we reached the fourth verse, the words struck me with the force of a hammer blow and sent tears to my eyes:

And should we die before our journey's through,

Happy day! All is well!

We then are free from toil and sorrow, too;

With the just we shall dwell!

But if our lives are spared again

To see the Saints their rest obtain,

Oh, how we'll make this chorus swell—

All is well! All is well!

And should we die before our journey's through. Those words penetrated deep into my heart, and I struggled to hold back my sobs. I knew that death was not the end. I knew that all would be resurrected through the Atonement of Jesus Christ. And while I didn't understand why God would allow the death of tiny babies, I knew that God had a plan for each of us, and that He would make every death right in the end. But despite knowing all this, I still felt overwhelmed with sadness. My grief didn't make any sense. I knew that this death was not real and that there was no actual baby in this little bundle. And I didn't even know the woman. But all the same, the pain I felt was deep. And I felt as if my heart was about to break.

There was a real sense of finality as we shovelled dirt into the hole and covered the tiny bundle. I was fighting back tears as I once again took my place at the front of the handcart. I couldn't rid my mind of that tragic image of the tear-streaked woman clutching the tiny bundle in her arms. I marvelled at how our brave pioneer women could possibly have found the strength to go on after losing their husbands and children and finding themselves all alone in the world. For me, it was enough to ponder. Steve, however, felt the need to do more.

"We need to go back," Steve exclaimed. "We need to invite her to join our family."

I could understand Steve getting a little caught up in the role play. She was a great actress, and she made the tragedy feel so real. I too had been deeply moved. However, I tried to bring Steve back to reality. "Steve, you know that woman is just acting!" I chided. "She doesn't want to join us. She wants to get back to the support crew camp where she'll be warm and comfortable."

"I know all this," Steve snapped. "But the whole point of trek is for us to act as the pioneers would have. And I know the pioneers would never have left this woman at the side of the road and just moved on. They would have taken her with them and made her part of their family."

I was about to object when Peter chipped in also. "He's right," Peter agreed. "We need to take her with us. It *is* what the pioneers would have done."

I looked at Mum and Dad for support. Dad looked at Steve and then Peter, his brow furrowing in thought. And then he just shrugged. With that encouragement Steve and Peter lowered the handcart and jogged back to the woman. Although I couldn't hear what they said to her, I saw the surprise flash over her face. She shook her head, but Steve kept on insisting. Eventually she reluctantly followed Steve and Peter. She walked like a prisoner towards her own execution. And this time the tears in her eyes were real.

"Family, this is Nancy," Steve declared proudly as he took his place again on the handcart. Nancy gave one final longing look at the spot that the support crew would have picked her up from and then began walking by our side, taking slow, unenthusiastic strides.

CHAPTER 7

On one level, I recognised that what Mum, Dad and I had sacrificed for the gospel's sake was nothing compared with what the pioneers had sacrificed. Burying that tiny bundle had very much driven that point home for me. All the same, my family had more in common with the pioneers than I first realised. Like the pioneers, we had given away all that we had and had even risked our very lives by embracing the gospel.

"Things aren't going so well," Dad had explained on that night that Paul and I had broken up. "The family aren't happy with the changes that they've seen in me. It's making them suspicious. Now that I'm living the gospel, I'm no longer any use to them. In fact, I'm now a liability. I know enough to put them all away, and in their minds I'm a risk that can't be tolerated."

Dad getting hurt had always been my worst fear, one that I tried very hard not to think about. I had friends who lost their fathers. Often their fathers just never came home after a night out and were never heard of again. Other men in the family got hurt, sometimes badly hurt. Gunshot wounds, stabbings, broken bones: these were all a part of everyday life in the mafia. I always tried to convince myself that it couldn't happen to my dad, but in my heart I knew that it really could. And it was probably just a matter of time before it did.

Suddenly my throat felt very dry. "So what are we going to do?" I asked hoarsely. Dad stroked his chin. "We have to leave. We need to disappear without a trace and start a new life."

It took a moment for me to grasp the enormity of what Dad was proposing. Sure, I had been willing to make some sacrifices for the gospel. But to leave our home? Our family? Our friends? This had never been part of the plan. I felt anger rise up from the pit of my stomach. "We can't just pack up and leave everything!" I retorted furiously. "We should never have invited the sister missionaries into our home. No one told me that listening to their message would result in us losing everything!"

"Or perhaps us gaining everything," Dad replied. "Jesus said, '*And every one that hath forsaken houses, or brethren, or sisters, or father, or mother, or wife, or children, or lands, for my name's sake, shall receive an hundredfold, and shall inherit everlasting life.*'" Dad looked me in the eye. "Chelsea, instead of setting our hearts on money and power, it's time we lived for things that really matter."

I sighed. Dad's mind was clearly made up. What was worse, I knew that Dad was right. "So when do we need to leave?" I asked apprehensively.

"Right now," Dad ordered. "Go upstairs. Pack everything that is important to you. Leave everything that's not. We need to leave in twenty minutes."

My jaw dropped open. Twenty minutes? A chill ran down my spine and penetrated deep into my heart as I considered how much danger we must be in if we had to leave in twenty minutes. I wouldn't have a chance to pack properly or to say goodbye to any of my friends. With a heavy heart, I trotted upstairs to my oversized bedroom.

I loved everything about my room. It was my very own place in the world, and words couldn't describe how much I abhorred the thought of leaving it all behind. I quickly grabbed my journal, my photos and my high school yearbook. I jammed my suitcases full of my favourite clothes and books. And that was about all that I could fit. I shut the door on my sound system, my shoes, my designer label clothing, my expensive perfumes, and all my other treasures. I had always enjoyed owning ten times more stuff than most girls my age. And now I barely owned anything.

Mum and Dad had already packed, so they were waiting for me. We marched out, and I miserably threw my suitcase into the trunk of our Mercedes Benz. "So where are we heading to, anyway?" I asked Dad grumpily. If I was expecting a detailed explanation, I was disappointed. Dad's response was more of a grunt than a meaningful reply. "Queensland," Dad muttered as he started the car.

It was late, and I dozed off in the back seat wondering and, to be honest, worrying what this new life would bring for us. My sleep was anything but peaceful, and I drifted into the most bizarre dream. I dreamt that I was Alice from Wonderland and that I was in the presence of the most beautiful white rabbit that I had ever seen. His eyes were huge and adorable, and they seemed to beckon me in and invite me to come closer. I approached the rabbit with an outstretched hand, but he fled once I got too close. I chased after the rabbit, begging for him to stop, and yet he just ignored my calls and darted down a rabbit hole. The hole was much too small for me, and yet I forced myself and somehow I managed to fit. I continued to pursue the rabbit. It was tight and dark, and I felt claustrophobic, but I forced myself through the crammed space. And then I had the rabbit cornered. I couldn't wait to pet this gorgeous rabbit who was staring at me with eyes as big as saucers, his nose twitching. Suddenly the rabbit snarled and pulled his lips back. Behind his lips was a row of razor-sharp teeth. I let out a terrified scream as the rabbit lunged at me. . .

I woke up with a start, my heart thundering in my ears. I was clammy with sweat, and I quickly wound down the window and let in a gust of chilly night air. I took in a few deep breaths as I waited for my pounding heartbeat to return to normal. I noticed that Dad was still driving, bathed in the glow of silvery moonlight. Mum had fallen fast asleep in the passenger seat. Dad looked exhausted. He looked like he might fall asleep right at the wheel.

"Dad, you need to get some sleep too," I told him. "Let me drive for a bit." Dad gratefully allowed me to take over. I adjusted my seat and mirror and accelerated down the highway. "So what happened?" I asked Dad. I now had him as a captive audience, and I was going to take advantage of the opportunity. "Why do you think they turned against you all of a sudden?"

We had an unwritten rule in our family that we never asked Dad about his life in the mafia. But I was sick of pretending that I didn't know what Dad did for a living. Dad sighed and for the first time ever gave me a straight answer about his mafia life. "They've been watching me change, Chelsea," Dad explained. "And it was making them suspicious. I overheard Carlos say that now that I had developed a conscience, maybe I would try to ease it by ratting on them. I could tell that the others were thinking the same thing. Once I saw the suspicion in their eyes, I knew that I wouldn't live out the week." I groaned. "Carlos really scares me," I confessed.

"You know what," Dad replied. "Me too."

Carlos was one of the really tough guys in our crime family. He had a reputation of being cruel and sadistic, and he was someone that you certainly didn't want to mess with. His nickname was "knife man", and I shuddered to think how he had earned that nickname. I don't think many people actually liked Carlos, but everyone respected him, and we certainly feared him. We all knew that if you get on the wrong side of Carlos, things ended very badly. If Dad was now on Carlos's bad side, we were definitely in a grave situation.

"Will we get to see Nana or Grandad again?" I asked Dad. "Or my aunties and uncles?"

"Someday," Dad reassured me, but he didn't sound convincing. "But right now no one can know where we are." Dad took his eyes of the road and looked me straight in the eye. "I'm serious about this, Chelsea," he said. "There is to be no contact with family or friends, and absolutely no contact with anyone from the mafia. Our lives depend on it!"

I nodded obediently. It felt funny to talk to Dad about these things. Up until recently, Dad had been more of an acquaintance than a father to me. He had spent his nights away with the mafia and his days sleeping. And there was the time that he had spent away from us in jail.

I opened my mouth to ask another question, but looking at Dad, I could see that he was distracted by something. I followed Dad's gaze and saw that he was staring intently into our rear-view mirror. I looked at the road behind us but didn't notice anything unusual. It was now the early hours of the morning, and the road was pretty deserted. There were just a handful of other cars on the highway. "Dad, what's wrong?" I asked. Dad lifted his shoulders in a little shrug. "We're being followed," he told me coolly.

CHAPTER 8

Nancy clearly wasn't coping well with being on trek. We were all tired and struggling, but Nancy was constantly sighing. She didn't even have to push the handcart, but she looked the unhappiest out of all of us. We had been travelling for half the day when Brother Lawson signalled for us to stop and set up camp. "Thank goodness," Nancy muttered loudly.

I was also really glad that we were stopping. My lack of sleep from the previous night was starting to take its toll. I took in a few deep breaths and filed my lungs with the fresh country air. We were now high in the hills, and the view was absolutely breathtaking. There were flat areas for sleeping and plenty of firewood, and there was a cool breeze, which is exactly what we needed on such a hot day.

"Jackson family, gather in!" Dad bellowed at us. We obediently gathered next to our handcart. "We need to get our camp ready," Dad ordered. "Bridget, Carly and Steve, I want you to help me to set up our shelter. Peter, Nancy and Chelsea, I want you to join the Brown family and help them dig a pit over there." Dad pointed out a spot about ten metres away.

"Why do we need a pit?" Nancy asked, frowning.

"For our toilets," Dad explained as he walked off. Bridget, Carly and Steve followed Dad, and I saw that Nancy's eyes were boring into the back of Steve's skull as he walked away. With a sigh, Nancy followed us to the Brown family. So far they hadn't got very far with their digging. We each picked up a shovel from the pile, and Nancy had an evil look on her face when she picked hers up.

Nancy may have been a whinger, but at least she worked hard. Soon the sweat was pouring down her face, but she continued to complain bitterly the whole time that she worked. "They had hot chocolate waiting for me back at the support crew camp," she whined to no one in particular. "My fiancé carries everything for me. And we don't even have to walk, let alone push handcarts. We drive everywhere we go. We have food and running water and real toilets that flush. I only agreed to go on trek because they told me it would be fun. No one said that I would be pushing handcarts and digging pits for toilets."

We just let Nancy vent. I figured that this was between her and Steve and Peter in any case. They were the ones who had twisted her arm to come with us. Nancy could just go back to the support crew for all I cared. Mum joined us a little while later and helped us to dig. "Don't worry," she whispered to me. "You're in for a treat. We're setting up for some pioneer games. After this, it will be fun for the rest of the day. "

And Mum was right. The rest of the day turned out to be a lot of fun. We began with a game where two people would sit on the ground facing each other and each holding onto the same stick. They would then both pull, and the stronger person would remain on the ground while the weaker person was pulled up. Peter did great in the boys' competition but was eventually defeated by a huge Samoan boy with massive arms.

We also jumped at the mark (which was a long jump without the run up) and had a three-legged race (which I did with Bridget and Marcia). However, the contest that I did best at was wrestling. To my great amazement, I found myself easily defeating the girls from the other families. The only other girl that did as well as me was Carly. This really surprised me, considering her slight frame. However, despite her delicate appearance, Carly was making mincemeat out of her opponents. The other girls each ended up on the ground in a cloud of dust. I figured that Carly must have had some training.

I was feeling happy when I faced off against Carly for my final match. Together we had done our family proud, and it really didn't matter to me whether I won or lost. Either way, it would have been a win for my family. However, when I looked over at Carly, I could see that she was taking this match much more seriously than I was. It clearly did matter to her which one of us won. As we faced off, I saw that she had a menacing expression on her face. "Get ready to get thrashed," she told me through gritted teeth. "I have a black belt in Judo, and I am going to put you through a world of pain."

At first I thought that Carly was being playful and that her threats were just banter. But as I looked at her again, I saw that her face was oozing hostility, and there was something about her mean, hard expression that sent a shiver down my spine. Suddenly I felt cold, even though the sun was warm on our backs.

As we began to wrestle, I was startled by Carly's aggression. She was putting everything into taking me out. Carly managed to grab my shoulder with her left hand. I pulled my head up in an effort to escape her grip, and Carly immediately took advantage of the opening. With a flurry of speed she stepped in, grabbed both of my legs behind the knee, and took me down.

I hit the ground hard, and the impact knocked the breath from my body. I immediately tried to regain control, but Carly now had the advantage. "Do you really think you can beat me?" she growled at me as we continued to wrestle on the ground. Carly's eyes narrowed to angry slits, and her face turned bright red as she moved to finish me off. My forehead dripped with sweat, and it took all my energy to stop Carly pinning me to the ground. I was exhausted and felt like just giving up and letting Carly win, but my pride made me hold on. A few minutes ago I hadn't cared which one of us won. Now, however, I was determined that I wouldn't let Carly get the better of me.

My heart pounded like crazy, and I was gasping for breath. While I had size on my side, Carly was much more skilled than I was and seemed to be able to manipulate every move I tried. It seemed hopeless. I tried everything, but nothing made Carly budge. She was clearly in control. And she was just watching and waiting for me to let my defences down so that she could finish me off.

And then I remembered a move that Dad had taught me. He thought that every girl should know basic self-defence in case she ever finds herself in a dangerous situation. "And it's even more important for a mafia girl," he had told me. "You have got to know how to get from a bad position to a good position. Knowing how to take care of yourself could someday be the difference between life and death."

I was certainly no expert in the martial arts, but I realised that one of the moves that Dad had taught me might be able to turn things around for me. The roar of the crowd faded into silence as I concentrated on my next move. I mustered up all of my strength, and a burst of adrenalin gave me the energy that I needed to push Carly's shoulder to the ground and press her arm straight across her back. I put pressure on her arm with everything that I had until Carly turned. And then I used my heavier weight to pin her to the ground.

I got up in a daze. I couldn't believe that I had actually managed to defeat Carly. As I stood up, I realised that all the youth were cheering and clapping for me. I was exhausted, but I was over the moon in having won this for my family. As the adrenalin faded, I realised how much my muscles ached. But I forgot all about my pain when Peter reached across and clasped my hand in his. "Well done, Chelsea!" he congratulated me with a big smile. I tried to reply, but I was still struggling to catch my breath. "Strong as well as beautiful I see," Peter remarked casually, and my heart skipped a beat. "Chelsea, you sure are full of surprises."

However not everyone was happy for me. Carly pushed her way through the crowd and stormed away, her face a mask of fury. She's pretty upset, I realised. She really wanted to beat me, and I wondered if I had just made an enemy. But I was too tired to care.

I guess that I had more mental strength than I gave myself credit for. I got a glimpse of my own inner strength on that night shortly after my family arrived in Brisbane following us fleeing from the mob life. Brisbane was a big, bustling city, and as we drove through the streets, I watched the crowds scurrying in every direction. Dad nodded his head towards the crowds as he drove. "One thing that I've learnt, Chelsea," he told me solemnly, "is that people are what really matter in life. I don't want to steal from people or hurt them anymore. Now, when I look at people, I just feel this overwhelming desire to make their lives better."

I was surprised when Dad parked on the street instead of turning into the hotel car park. I looked at Dad questioningly. "This car can be traced back to us," Dad explained, "I don't want anyone to see us with it." Dad ran a hand through his hair and reached into his jacket and pulled out an envelope. "Here is everything we need," he told us, his face taut. "I have drivers licences for Mum and I. . . birth certificates. . . everything in our new names. From now on I'm Jeff Jackson and Mum is Maria. Chelsea, I've let you keep your name. I don't want you to get confused and let your real name slip. Mum and I are more experienced in using false identities than you are. Just remember that your last name now is Jackson".

"Just let Mum and I do the talking," Dad muttered to me as we approached the counter. They both looked calm and unruffled, and I wondered how many times Dad and Mum had used false identities before. When we were done, Dad handed Mum and me the keys to our rooms and walked off without a word. I looked at Mum questioningly. "Dad needs to get rid of the car," Mum whispered in my ear.

I made myself comfortable in my room and switched on the TV. What would Dad do with the car? I wondered as I stretched out on the bed, my arms folded behind my head. I pictured him pushing it into a lake like you see in the movies but decided that that wouldn't make any sense. The car was registered in Dad's name, and so simply dumping it would raise questions once it was found. I figured that Dad must have something else in mind. Whatever it was, I wouldn't be asking any questions.

When Dad came back, we all went out for burgers and milkshakes together. Everything had been so tense since we went on the run, but as we went out for dinner together as a family, I found myself relaxing for the first time. I felt so much better with a good meal in my stomach and began to feel a little more optimistic about the future. Although we had just lost everything, I felt in my heart that everything was going to be alright.

We were all feeling more cheerful and at ease when we returned to the hotel. However, our carefree mood quickly evaporated when Dad suddenly lifted his finger to his lips and gestured to Mum and me to stay behind him. I felt a flood of adrenaline rush through my body, and my breath caught in my throat. Dad had obviously sensed some danger that I was not even aware of. I reminded myself that I could not let my guard down. While it had been nice to switch off for an hour, I scolded myself for getting too comfortable and not remaining alert. Danger really could be around any corner.

Dad silently approached his hotel room door and pushed it open in a swift motion. I exhaled and let my body relax a little when I saw that the room was dark and empty. Everything seemed normal to me, and I wondered what Dad had been concerned about. "Dad, what is it?" I called out breathlessly. Dad arched a brow and switched on the lights. My heart missed a beat when I saw two men in dark suits and ties sitting on the sofa. What on earth? I thought. They must have just been sitting in the dark, waiting for us. Mum just stood there, frozen in fear, a look of absolute terror on her face. My heart began to pound wildly as the two men stood up and one of them reached into his suit jacket. This is it, I thought. We did our best to get away, but they have caught up with us. I waited for the man to pull out a gun. And I braced myself for the shots that would end our lives.

CHAPTER 9

At first I was terrified. I was more frightened than I had ever been before in my life. My heart began racing furiously, and adrenaline flooded through me. My whole body tensed as I realised I was about to be shot. I wanted to do something, but I knew that we were completely at their mercy. What will that feel like? I wondered. I hoped that it would be quick and painless. I didn't want to experience the agony of death as my life slowly drained from my body. All of a sudden I felt nauseous, and the room began to spin. This can't be happening to us, I thought. But then I looked over at Dad and saw that he looked calm, almost nonchalant. And I decided that if Dad could look death squarely in the eye, then I would too. I was petrified, but I wanted to die well like my dad. More than anything, I wanted Dad to be proud of me in our final moments. And so I put on a defiant face and waited for the man to pull out his gun. But instead he pulled out a badge. "I'm Sergeant Alvarado, and this is Inspector Leach", he told us. "We're from the New South Wales Police Organised Crime Squad."

I exhaled deeply and offered up a silent prayer of thanks. I was overwhelmed with relief and gratitude. While the police's presence probably meant trouble for us, I welcomed that trouble with open arms. I still felt weak at the knees and leaned against a wall to steady myself. This certainly wasn't the first time that the police had come by for an unexpected visit. Dad never seemed flustered when the police knocked on our door. He was always cool and polite, and he exemplified that same politeness now.

"Gentlemen, why don't you take a seat," Dad invited, gesturing with his hand, and Sergeant Alvarado and Inspector Leach sat back down, looking uncomfortable. "Look," Sergeant Alvarado told my Dad "We know that you've had some kind of mid-life crisis and that you're trying to change your life. If you're serious about giving up a life of crime, good on ya. But you should know that your people aren't very happy that you've left. If we were able to track you down, how long do you think it will take them to find you?"

"Yes, I thought someone was following us while we were driving up here," Dad told the officers.

"That's right," Inspector Leach confirmed. "We were watching your home when you left. We followed your car down here. The family, however, have no idea where you went to. *Yet.*" Inspector Leach emphasised the "yet."

"But they're pretty unhappy," Sergeant Alvarado continued. "You know that no one ever leaves the family." It was true; we certainly did know that. I had heard stories of those who had tried to leave. It never ended well for them.

"But we have an idea," Inspector Leech interjected and then paused to make sure that he had our attention. Dad nodded for him to go on. "What we suggest is that you return to your family and tell them that you just needed to get away for a few days. Then go back to your life as a member of the mafia but become a police informer."

Inspector Leach paused again and waited for Dad to say something. Dad leaned back in his chair but didn't say a word. After an awkward silence Inspector Leach continued talking. "Of course we'd pay you," he added. "If you're serious about doing the right thing from now on, you'd help us. You'd be protecting people for a change. You'd become one of the good guys."

Dad snorted in disgust. "Let's get this straight," he demanded, his voice rising in anger. "Now that I've finally left my old life, you want me to become part of that life again? Do you seriously expect me to go back and act like nothing has happened? Do you really want me to continue to live the life of a criminal?"

"If you're serious about doing the right thing, then you would do this." Inspector Leech retorted. "You would be helping us to stop crime and protect the community. You would be doing a very good thing."

"Fellas, what I really need to do now is protect my family," Dad explained patiently. The anger had disappeared from his voice, and he was once again his calm, collected self. "That means not only protecting them from the mafia but also protecting them from being around their influence. I can't be a part of that life anymore. Even if I go back with the best of intentions, that lifestyle will corrupt me. I can't be part of that life and be the man that I need to be."

Inspector Leach nodded. "We understand, John," he said gently. "And we wish you all the best. But we have to warn you, John. Just because you don't want to be part of that life anymore doesn't mean that they are going to let you leave. Be careful, John. They are after you."

CHAPTER 10

It felt like déjà vu. After another bitter and cold night with too little food in our stomachs, too little time in front of the campfire and too much time shivering in our sleeping bags completely unable to sleep, the new day saw us once again pushing handcarts in the frosty first light of dawn. A dingo howled somewhere in the distance, and the hairs stood up on the back of my neck.

It was now mid-morning, and I sighed as the handcart in front of us stopped for the umpteenth time. The Brown family were struggling to keep pushing, and our progress was really slowing down because of them. "What's going on with them?" I muttered angrily. I knew that I should be more patient, but exhaustion was making me irritable. It took much more energy to keep on stopping and starting than it would have taken to keep moving.

I used the break to wipe my forehead with my sleeve. As I glanced over at the river bank, I saw something that made my blood run cold. There was a tall, wiry man on the other side of the river. And he was staring right at me. His hands were thrust into his trouser pockets, and he had a look of coolness and distance on his face.

An icy feeling of dread crept over my spine, and I felt my throat tighten. I just stood there, frozen like a statue. I felt his eyes boring down on me, and it gave me the creeps. Was I just imagining that he was staring? I wondered. It was still foggy, and I couldn't make the man out perfectly. But I could see him clearly enough, and he was definitely staring in our direction.

Is it really any wonder that he's staring? I tried to reassure myself. How often do you see a bunch of teenagers in nineteenth-century clothing pushing handcarts when you go for a walk in the bush? But it still didn't add up, and I couldn't shake the feeling that there was something seriously wrong. The man was wearing a dark, pin-striped suit with a silk tie. And he wasn't staring at us as a group. He was staring directly at me.

I again cast my eyes in the direction of the man, and this time our eyes met. I felt a stab of fear as the man shot me an evil look, his eyes glowing with hatred. Who could this man be? I wondered. My heart continued to pound as I searched my memory. But I couldn't think straight. Fear clouded my mind and began to choke my throat. I didn't recognise the man, but I was terrified that our past may have caught up with us.

My attention was diverted away from the man as my back began itching like crazy. I twisted and began scratching furiously. Bridget looked over at me curiously. "Why on earth are you scratching like that?" she asked.

"I don't know what it is," I said as I continued scratching. "But I'm just really itchy all of a sudden." The itch had distracted me from the man for a moment, but I was now keen to get another look at him. However, to my surprise he was no longer there. The river bank was empty where the man had been standing just moments earlier.

I tried not to think about the man as we began moving again. It wasn't hard to distract myself as I was now beginning to itch all over. Soon the itching was unbearable. I was now scratching with one hand while pushing the handcart with the other hand. "I just can't stop scratching," I explained to Bridget. "Neither can I," Bridget replied, and I saw that she was also scratching away furiously.

Soon everyone in our family was scratching themselves every chance that they could get. We kept on dropping the handcart so that we could scratch ourselves and get a moment's relief from the maddening itch. Dad reached over and pulled up Peter's shirt, and to my shock I saw horrible little bugs embedded in Peter's flesh and sucking his blood. "We've all got ticks," Dad explained and quickly took charge. "Okay, boys, go over that hill over there. Girls, stay here. Let's check each other and get rid of them before we all tear our own skins off".

I paired off with Bridget, and we began to examine each other. Bridget found five ticks on me, and I found three on Bridget. It made my skin crawl to think of these tiny, little bugs crawling all over my skin and sucking my blood. Trek was certainly turning out to be a difficult experience, I thought. But I was grateful that I was experiencing it with a friend like Bridget. Having a friend like her with me made the whole experience much easier, and I was so glad that Bridget had arranged for us to be in the same family. I suddenly felt an overpowering sense of gratitude as I realised that Bridget had been there for me during so many difficult times in my life. Like an angel, she had come into my life when I was feeling alone and confused and scared, and she had lit up my darkest moments.

I had tried so hard to throw myself into my new life following our move to Brisbane, but it wasn't working. The spirit was willing, but the flesh was weak, and I was suffering withdrawal symptoms from my old life. I felt as if my whole life had been turned upside down, and I was left feeling empty, lonely and sad. After we found an apartment to rent, I just spent a couple of days in my room listening to music. I could tell that Mum and Dad were getting worried about me, but I didn't care. I just wanted to mope around and feel sorry for myself. Mum and Dad, however, had other ideas, and before I knew it, they had enrolled me at the local high school.

"I don't understand why I have to go to school here," I told Mum and Dad irritably. "I mean, we're probably not going to be here very long, are we? It's not like this is going to be our home. We've got nothing but the clothes on our backs."

"Chelsea, we don't know how long we're going to be here," Dad had explained. "Maybe we'll go someplace else. Maybe we'll stay here. But I'm not having you sit at home all day," he told me firmly.

I continued to complain to Mum as she dragged me along to the local high school to get me enrolled. "Chelsea, changing our lives is not easy," she told me, "and we're not going to be able to do it if we leave gaps in our lives. This isn't the first time that your Dad has tried to change his life. But every time your Dad has tried in the past, he's fallen back into his old ways. You see, you can't just base change on emptying bad things out of your life. If you really want to change, you need to fill your life with good things and start filling those gaps. In your case, this means that you'll be going to school and studying hard."

It was miserable starting school partway through the term, especially in such a large school. In the past I had always felt so secure at school. I hung out with the other mafia kids and felt invincible in their company. No one dared to mess with us, and it seemed that we always got whatever we wanted. Now I was just a nobody lost in the crowd. I didn't have a person in the world that I could trust or who even seemed to notice me. I might as well have been invisible.

I longed so much for someone to invite me into their circle and befriend me, but no one did. I wandered around the school during my first lunch and watched the different groups, but I could tell that I didn't really fit in with any of them. Eventually I gave up and went to the school library so I could read the one book that had always brought me comfort during my hard times. And as I read the Book of Mormon, a sense of peace enveloped me like a warm blanket on a cold winter's night, and I felt comforted. And it put things into perspective for me. I decided that if Moroni could survive all those years wandering alone in the wilderness while being hunted by his enemies, then I could survive starting the school year midway through.

I spent every lunch that week in the library reading the Book of Mormon on my own. By the time Friday came around, I was still feeling lonely and quite sorry for myself when I saw that a tall, elegant-looking girl with long, curly blond hair and vivid blue eyes was making her way towards me. "Wow, I thought it was the Book of Mormon that you were reading," she exclaimed cheerfully. "Are you a Mormon?"

"Why do you want to know?" I asked suspiciously. I didn't want to be made fun of for reading the Book of Mormon alone in the library. But the girl didn't seem like a bully to me. Her eyes were friendly and she had a kind expression on her face. In any case, her reply put me at ease. "Well, I'm a member of The Church of Jesus Christ of Latter-day Saints myself," she told me, "and I thought that you might also be a member of the church."

I smiled. Maybe my luck was going to change after all. It felt so good to meet a member of the church. Although I didn't even know this girl, meeting her felt like coming home. "Well, no, I'm not," I explained to her. "That is, I haven't been baptised as yet. I'm just learning about the church at this stage."

"That's great!" the girl told me excitedly. "I tell you, that book can change your life!" The girl held out her hand warmly. "I'm Bridget," she said.

"I'm Chelsea," I replied, grasping her hand firmly.

"So, do you normally hang out at the library at lunch time?" Bridget asked me.

"No," I said defensively. "Do you?"

"Nah," Bridget replied. "I just had to look a few things up for an assignment. But I've got the information that I need now. Do you want to join me and my friends for lunch?"

And that was my first lunch with my new friends. Bridget introduced me to a tall, pretty Irish girl with fiery red hair named Leah and a Tongan girl with straight black hair and piercing dark eyes named Mele. Leah was a bubbly and cheerful girl who immediately launched into a series of questions. "So where are you from?" she asked me curiously. I was about to tell my new friends that I was from Sydney, but then I remembered that I needed to protect my family's identity. I decided that the fewer truthful details that I provided about myself, the better. "I'm from Melbourne," I lied.

"Oh, I used to live in Melbourne when we first came to Australia. What part of Melbourne?"

I chided myself for my stupid lie. I really didn't know anything about Melbourne. As I searched my mind for a believable answer, I remembered that I had a cousin whose family was part of the mafia in Melbourne. What was the name of the suburb that they lived in? "Doncaster," I replied.

"Oh, that's not far from where I used to live. I'm from Box Hill".

This wasn't going well. I decided that it was time to change the subject before I got a question that I couldn't answer. "So you're all members of the church?" I asked the group.

"Yeah, we're the only members of the church in our school," Leah replied. "So what is the deal with you?"

"The missionaries were teaching my family while we lived in. . . Melbourne." I had almost said Sydney, but I caught myself in time. "We probably would have been baptised there but we had to move. . . for my Dad's work."

"Oh, yeah, where does your Dad do for work?" Leah inquired.

"You ask a lot of questions!" I snapped. "Why are you putting me through the third degree?"

"Sorry," Leah blurted, turning red. She looked confused by my sudden outburst. "I didn't mean to pry."

I felt embarrassed by my reaction, and I knew that I had come across as rude. But at least that was better than letting our identity slip. That was something that could get us all killed. However one thing was clear to me. I would have to get together with Mum and Dad and we would all have to get our story straight.

CHAPTER 11

"It's such a great movie," Peter told Steve and Carly as we pushed the handcart. The wind was blowing noisily, and Peter had to raise his voice above it. "And man, that girl in it, she's so hot!" My back was aching from all the pushing, and I felt a tightness in my neck. We were all tired and sore, and I figured that Peter was just trying to lighten the mood. And I guess it worked. Soon our family was laughing, and everyone was feeling a little more light-hearted. All the same, it just didn't feel right to me. Even as a recent convert to the church, I could tell that this movie wasn't up to our standards. I hadn't seen it, but from Peter's description it was clearly full of immorality, crudeness and violence. I thought someone would say something, but the others didn't seem to be bothered by the conversation. In fact Steve and Carly were hanging on Peter's every word. I exchanged a meaningful glance with Bridget, and I could tell that she wasn't impressed with the direction of this conversation.

I looked over at Mum and Dad to see if they would do anything, but they were acting as if they hadn't even heard the conversation. During our break I made my way over to a stream and washed the grime from my face. From the water's edge I heard Dad's voice calling for us to gather in.

"When Brigham Young was leading the pioneers across the plains," Dad began, "a lot of the pioneers were doing the wrong thing. They were quarrelling, gambling, being lazy and sometimes even getting drunk. And so President Young gathered them around and warned them that they could not build Zion if they embraced evil at the same time.

He told them that they were not just looking for a place to settle, but that God had a higher and holier purpose for them. And it is the same with us. I know that God has a higher purpose for each of our lives, and we just all need to live up to our higher purposes."

Nothing further needed to be said after that. Peter, Steve and Carly gave each other guilty looks and stared at the ground. Dad's words also touched me, and I committed to myself that I would be cleaner and more spiritual from now on. I decided that I wanted to live up to my higher purpose.

Brother Lawson came over to Dad while we were resting and whispered something to him. I looked over at them curiously. Brother Lawson's manner was still cold and aloof, and I could sense the hostility between the two of them. After Brother Lawson had left, Dad gathered us together. "Okay, we're now going to do a silent pull," Dad explained to us. "That means that no one is allowed to speak until I say you can. I want you to use this time to ponder about whatever you think is most important, or whatever you feel prompted to."

At first, the silence felt really awkward. I shivered as we pulled. The afternoon was turning cold, and my nose was beginning to run. I sniffed back the dribbles and began to think about my life. As I silently pondered, I found myself really enjoying the stillness and the solitude. Soon I was hearing sounds and seeing things that I had never noticed before. I was absorbing the beauty of our surroundings. The trees, the hills, the kangaroos, the wild flowers, the clouds in the sky: they all had God's imprint on them. Our goal to reach Zion was surely a noble and lofty goal, but Heavenly Father seemed to be whispering to me that life was as much about the journey as the destination. And I felt strongly that He wanted me to have joy in the journey.

As I pondered, all of a sudden I felt warm all over, as if someone was hugging me. And at that moment I felt as if my Heavenly Father was close by, and that He knew who I was, and that He cared deeply about me. For a moment it felt like it was just God and I. I felt as if God, the Creator of the universe, and His obscure, insignificant daughter were having a moment together. And despite my insignificance, I felt as if God loved me, and as if I was the whole world to Him. I wanted that moment to last forever, and I hoped the silent pull would go all day. However, I was thrown back into the real world when I noticed that all of the handcarts ahead of us had halted.

"What's going on?" I whispered to Bridget. I was whispering since I wasn't sure if we were actually allowed to talk as yet. Bridget just shrugged. Soon Brother Lawson came up to us. "We are dangerously short on supplies," Brother

Lawson roared. "We need all the men to rise up and help us hunt."

Dad, Peter and Steve gave us a wave goodbye and followed Brother Lawson and the other men over the hill, and Mum took over Peter's place on the handcart. With alarm I realised that this meant that us women would have to pull the handcarts all by ourselves. How long would the boys be off for? I wondered. I really hoped that it wouldn't be too long.

We did our best, but it was so hard pushing the handcart all by ourselves. I didn't realise how much of a load Peter and Steve had been taking off the rest of us. We struggled and did our best, but I couldn't wait for the boys to return. The hours that we were pushing the handcart by ourselves seemed to drag on forever.

I realised that things were going to get much worse once we approached the base of the biggest hill that we had yet come across on trek. We can't get up that, I thought. There's no way we are going to be able to push this handcart up that hill without the boys. I looked over at Bridget and saw that she had a worried expression on her face. The organisers planned this on purpose, I thought angrily. They deliberately saved the steepest hill for when the women were pushing the handcarts on their own. They want to see us fail.

Sensing our low spirits, Mum called out encouragements to us. "You can do this, girls!" she told us cheerfully, "Let's go!" At first I was irritated by Mum's encouragements. Can't she see that this is too hard for us? I thought angrily. But my heart softened as I remembered the powerful experience I had just had during the silent pull. Yes, I can do this, I decided, and I would do it for my Heavenly Father. I would prove that I could do hard things without complaining.

We mustered up all our strength and courage and began pushing with all our might. We ran at first. However, when we reached what we thought was the top of the hill, we realised that we were only halfway there and that the peak was still further ahead. Nancy was heaving and sweating by now, and she shot us an angry glare. I knew what she was thinking. "Hey, don't look at me," I snapped at her. "I didn't make you join us. This is between you and Steve."

It was beginning to hurt so much, but I pushed on through the pain. My breath was coming in short, sharp gasps. As we got a little closer to the top, I saw a sight that touched me deeply. All the young men were standing at the top of the hill. They were all watching us. Their expressions were pained, and I saw respect in their eyes. They had all taken off their hats and were holding them in their hands. I searched for Peter's face, and my eyes fixed on his as we pushed past. Peter smiled at me. And then I collapsed in front of him.

CHAPTER 12

I slowly opened my eyes and saw that Mum and Dad were looking down at me with worried expressions on their faces. I groaned and tried to lift up my head, but I immediately felt nauseous, so I laid my head down again. Mum gently brushed my fringe out of my eyes and felt my forehead. "Chelsea, are you all right?" she asked, and her voice was tender with concern. At first I was too disorientated to answer. I didn't even know where I was. All that I knew was that I was far from home. Slowly the events of the past few days came flooding back to me: coming on trek, nearly drowning in the river, being knocked over by the member of the mob, wrestling Carly, and finally the women's pull. Dad smiled down and nodded at me. "I'm really proud of you, pushing yourself like that."

I looked over at Bridget, Carly and Nancy. They were all sweaty and still catching their breath. I noticed, however, that Carly had an odd expression on her face. She flashed me an insincere smile. "For a moment I thought we lost you," she said snidely, and she seemed almost happy about it. I frowned, and I felt my face burning hot. What does

Carly have against me? I wondered. I held Carly's gaze until Peter coughed with unease.

"Yeah, we couldn't let anything happen to you," Peter interjected, trying to break the awkward confrontation. Mum and Dad exchanged meaningful glances. I turned away from Carly and looked down from the top of the hill. The view was breathtaking, and I couldn't believe that we had come so far. I tried to stand up, but I felt weak at the knees, and a violent wave of nausea rushed though my body. Peter caught me in his arms as my body folded down to the ground. I was too tired to exert myself any further, and so I just let him set me down on the ground.

Dad put his hand on my shoulder. "Would you like a blessing?" Dad asked me. I nodded weakly, and Dad called over Brother Semmler to anoint me with oil. Dad then sealed the anointing, and as he did so, I felt of the love that my Heavenly Father has for me. Dad told me that Heavenly Father was pleased with me and promised that I would recover and have all the strength that I needed to complete trek. He told me that I would learn lessons on trek that would be with me for the rest of my life, and that I would build memories that I would treasure forever. He finally promised that I would always be glad that I came on trek.

I felt my strength returning following the blessing, but Dad once again insisted that I walk next to the handcart instead of pushing. "I'm fine now," I argued. "It will be easy now that we have the boys again." But Dad wouldn't have a bar of it. "Why do you keep on making me walk?" I asked in exasperation. "Quit drowning and collapsing," Dad retorted, "and then I'll quit making you walk beside the handcart."

The sun was beginning to sink in the sky, and as the night fell, so did the temperature. No matter how hot it got during the day, the nights were always freezing. We would sweat all day and burn under the blazing sun and then spend all night shivering and trying to get warm. I watched enchanted as the night sky began to glitter with stars and the moon cast its cold, silver light all over us. You could see the stars so much more clearly here than you could in the city. Mum and Dad were holding each other's hands as they walked beside the handcart, which was really nice to see. It was the first time I ever recall them showing affection in public.

At first the night was still and quiet. All that you could hear was the crunch of the handcart's wheels as it was pushed over the leafy ground. However, we soon began to hear strange noises all around us in the bush. A sharp wind began to howl around us, causing the branches of the gum trees to creak. My heart began beating quickly when I heard a rustling in the bushes just behind us. I quickly spun my head around, but I couldn't see anything.

Peter looked over at me, and saw that I looked worried. "Don't worry," he assured me. "It's probably just some animal." I could tell that he was trying to sound cheerful. But I was worried. The night had been so beautiful just a short time ago. Now it felt heavy with my fear.

Suddenly the hairs stood up on the back of my neck as I heard a rustling in the bushes ahead of us. My eyes darted to the bushes, but there was no one there. Stop it, I told myself sternly; there's nothing to be afraid of. I convinced myself that I was just working myself up into a state and letting my imagination run away with me.

I held my breath as I squinted into the darkness at the bushes. I realised that my heart was pounding and that I was breathing heavily. I looked over again, and this time I thought I saw a figure in the bushes. It looked like some kind of beast. I felt a knot beginning to form in the pit of my stomach. I knew that this was trouble.

Suddenly I heard a deep, resonating bark. We all stumbled to a halt, and I edged as close as I could to my family. We all paused, and I listened hard. I couldn't hear anything but my beating heart.

"What is it?" Mum asked, barely breathing. Dad dropped Mum's hand and stared warily ahead. Suddenly

Peter began pointing. I raised my eyes but didn't see anything except dark shadows. We cautiously began to creep the handcart forward in the direction that Peter was pointing, making as little noise as we could. I nearly jumped out of my skin when a large, shadowy figure jumped right out in front of our handcart. I opened my mouth and screamed.

CHAPTER 13

My eyes opened wide with fear. As I stared, I could see that the shadowy figure was a dingo. In a second we were surrounded by other dingos, their thick fur on end. The dingos' teeth were bared, and they were snarling viciously. Their red eyes gleamed in the darkness, and then those red eyes began to move in on us.

My throat tightened in panic. The lead dingo opened its jaws widely and bared its teeth, its eyes rolled back in its head. Carly screamed so loudly it made my ears hurt. Gritting his teeth, Peter let go of the handcart and charged at the beasts. "No, Peter, don't!" I yelled after him, but Peter ignored me. Peter aimed a big kick at the chest of the lead dog. The kick struck it with incredible force and sent the dingo sprawling.

Bridget uttered a shriek as one of the dingos took a big lunge at Peter. A set of sharp teeth ripped into Peter's arm, and Peter's eyes bulged in alarm as a snarling, sandy figure pulled him to the ground. Dad ran to Peter's aid and helped him struggle to his feet, and the two of them then fended of the dingos as best as they could.

My eyes flickered around, looking for anything that might help us, and I saw a stick that we could use as a club. Should I go for it, I wondered? I knew that we really shouldn't get separated. But all the same, arming ourselves seemed like the best option at the moment. My entire body was trembling and my heart pounding like crazy as I ran for the stick. I was running as fast as I could, but all the same my legs felt like they were made out of lead. "Chelsea, no!" Mum called out after me. "We can't get separated." "Chelsea!" Steve also called out after me in a tiny, weak voice. Steve was clearly terrified, but all the same, he ran to my aid.

I knew that running for the stick was a foolish move and that I was putting myself in danger. But I couldn't just stand there and wait for the dingos to tear Dad and Peter to pieces. I had to do something. As I had hoped, two of the dingos separated from the pack and chased after me, but I managed to grab the stick before they got to me. I danced out of the way as they growled and snapped at me.

I held the stick firmly in front of me, but my hands were shaking too much to aim well. I swung my club hard at the first dingo's head, but the dingo dodged it easily. Pouncing forward, the dingo took a lunge at my wrist, its razor-sharp teeth barely missing. I swung again at the dog, and this time the dingo caught my club in its teeth and ripped it from my hands.

This is it, I thought. A wave of fear swept over me as I realised that Steve and I were now defenceless and completely at the dingos' mercy. Just then I heard a loud gunshot in the air, and the dingos fled in terror. I looked over and saw that Brother Lawson was standing there, holding a rifle. "It's just a blank," he told us casually. "I was going to use it for a scenario later on."

A flood of relief swept over me. My hero! I thought. Brother Lawson has just saved all of us. "Thank you!" I blurted out gratefully, running up to Brother Lawson. "I thought that we were in real trouble there."

I was expecting at least a gracious response. We had been terrified, and Peter had just been bitten. However, Brother Lawson's reaction was cold and bitter. He didn't ask us if we were all right or show us any concern. Rather, he immediately reprimanded us. "I shouldn't have to be running off to rescue you lot," Brother Lawson told us bitterly. "You shouldn't even be here. You don't deserve to be here."

I felt like I had just been slapped in the face, and resentment began rising from the pit of my stomach. What on earth does this man have against us? I wondered. He's pathetic, I thought angrily. He's just a pathetic, bitter man. "You're such a hypocrite," I shot back at him. "You act like you're such a good person, but you're mean to me and my family for no reason. I know that God has forgiven me. What right do you have to judge me?"

I didn't expect my outburst to have any effect on Brother Lawson, but Brother Lawson all of a sudden looked like he had been struck. "You're right", he said in a tiny, breaking voice. "I'm sorry. . ."

"Well, you're not all wrong," Dad told him candidly. "I am a criminal and a thug. There's nothing about me that is noble. But I'm trying really hard to change."

I was stunned by Dad's confession. Dad never opened up about our past and was obsessed with protecting our identities. I remember how alarmed he was when I confessed that I had told my friends that I was from Doncaster. "I really wished you hadn't told them that," he scolded me. "We don't even know Melbourne. When you lie, you should always create a story about something you're familiar with. That way, if someone asks you questions, you will be able to answer them convincingly."

"That's the thing, Dad," I exclaimed irritably, "I don't want to lie. And I don't want to have to try and remember the things that I lie about. I don't want to have to worry about being caught out."

Dad sighed. "I know, Chelsea," he said. "I don't want that for you either. But for the moment we need to do this to make sure that we're all safe." He turned to Mum. "We're all going to have to get to know Doncaster in case we're asked any questions," he told us. "We can learn a lot from the internet."

That Sunday we attended church as a family. I was excited to go to church since I knew that Bridget would be there. As we arrived, I noticed that our ward in Brisbane was a lot like the ward that we had attended in Sydney. The car park was full of station wagons and minivans, and I noticed that the members all acted like they were one close family. Everyone seemed to know each other and to be friendly to each other.

I saw Bridget talking to Leah and Mele as I walked into the chapel. A big grin spread across Bridget's face as she saw me. Next thing I knew, Bridget was at my side, and she threw her arms around me in a big hug.

Although I was warmed by Bridget's reception, being at church still felt strange and uncomfortable to me. My

feelings of discomfort, however, began to fade as the con-
gregation began to sing the opening hymn.

I have a family here on earth.

They are so good to me.

I want to share my life with them

through all eternity.

Families can be together forever

through Heavenly Father's plan.

I always want to be with my own family,

And the Lord has shown my how I can.

The Lord has shown my how I can.

As I listened to these words, I felt a tingling all over,
and I was enveloped with warmth. Cherish your family,
the spirit whispered to me. Love your parents, watch out
for them, and follow their guidance. Suddenly I felt overwhelmed with feelings of love for my parents. I looked
over at them with fresh eyes. Mum was singing with a rich,
beautiful voice and was pouring her whole heart into wor-
shiping her Heavenly Father. While Dad wasn't signing as
loudly, he had a look of reverence and sincerity on his face.
I could tell that he was at peace at church and happy to be
there. At that moment, as I watched my parents, I caught a
glimpse of the way that Heavenly Father sees them.

Once the meeting was over, Dad introduced himself
to the missionaries. "The sister missionaries were teaching

us the discussions in Melbourne," Dad explained, "but we moved before we could be baptised. Could you please continue to teach us?" The elders just looked at each other in amazement. I'm guessing that this didn't happen very often.

I loved being taught the final missionary discussions. Now that we had actually left our old lives, we listened to the discussions with a commitment and an intensity that we hadn't had before. Despite having put my whole heart into the gospel message, I was still feeling apprehensive as we all drove down to the chapel for our baptismal interview with the zone leader. Elder Cowell turned out to be a jolly, outgoing missionary with a kind face. He was able to immediately put me at ease with his friendliness and his sense of humour. I felt at peace and was able to answer his questions with the assurance that I had done my best to live all the standards that had been taught to me, and I knew that God had accepted my offering.

"Sure," I told Elder Cowell when he asked me to explain what the word of wisdom was. "It means that we don't smoke, do drugs, or drink alcohol, tea of coffee. I'm committed to live this commandment." Elder Cowell nodded approvingly. "And what does the church teach about sex before marriage?" he asked next. "That it's not on," I said simply.

"You're all ready to be baptised, Chelsea" Elder Cowell told me once the interview was over. "Congratulations!"

I was so excited and so happy. I waited out in chapel foyer as Mum and Dad had their interviews. Mum was beaming when she came out of her interview. She seemed to be just radiating light and happiness. Dad's interview, however, took much longer than what I had expected. I grew restless as the minutes just ticked by. "Why is it taking so long?" I asked Mum after I had checked my watch for the fifth time. Mum and I exchanged worried glances.

As soon as Dad walked out of his interview, I could tell that something was wrong. Dad looked downcast and disappointed, and I knew immediately that his interview had not gone smoothly. I really felt for him. Dad had changed his whole life for the gospel's sake. He had given up everything that he had and had put both his own life and our lives in danger. I knew how much being baptised meant to him.

Elder Cowell went back into the room by himself. "It looks like I'm going to have to be interviewed by the mission president," Dad explained. "Elder Cowell is calling him now."

The wait continued, and I got up and began pacing the foyer while Mum put her hand over Dad's. Elder Cowell came out about fifteen minutes later. "I'm sorry," Elder

Cowell told Dad. "President Dunne won't be able to come down until Tuesday next week, so we're going to have to postpone Saturday's baptism." I was bitterly disappointed that I wasn't able to be baptised that coming Saturday after all, but I wanted us all to do this together as a family.

We were soon to be disappointed again. After the mission president interviewed Dad, he told him that he would have to seek the First Presidency's permission for Dad to be baptised. This took a long time, and we tried our best to get on with our lives while we were waiting. I tried to distract myself with school work and soon found myself getting good marks for the first time ever in my life. Eventually Dad got a call from Elder Cowell. I could tell that it was good news by Dad's tone while he spoke to him. Dad's tone usually didn't give much away, but Dad sounded distinctly happy. And he was thanking Elder Cowell profusely. "Everything has been approved," Dad told us cheerfully after he hung up the phone. "We can all be baptised this Saturday."

I loved the photo that Elder Hedley took of us in front of the meetinghouse. Mum, Dad and I were all dressed in white, and standing together, we felt like a real family. But it broke my heart that Sister Green and Sister Lata didn't even know that we were being baptised. They would have been so happy, but they didn't even know what happened to us. We had just disappeared on them without any kind of explanation. I really hoped that someday the danger would pass and I could give them the happy news. I wanted them to know that they had forever changed our lives, and to thank them for coming on a mission and for knocking on our door.

The baptismal service was beautiful. It felt special to have my best friend give the talk on baptism and to be baptised together with Mum and Dad.

Although I felt a light and a joy in my life following my baptism that I had never before experienced, I still had my struggles as a new convert. I came from a very different life than the other girls at church, and, with the exception of Bridget, I never felt like I fitted in with the other girls. However Bridget's unconditional love always made me feel accepted. Bridget was so caring and concerned during my early months in the church. In time I began to feel comfortable not just around Bridget but with her other friends also.

CHAPTER 14

It was freezing cold as soon as the sun went down. Even with my gloves on, I felt the chilling cold numbing my fingers. I think that was why Dad was so confused when I asked if we could go without a fire that night.

"Why on earth would you want to go without a fire on a night like tonight?" Dad exclaimed in disbelief. And so I explained about the person that I had seen watching me. "I'm just worried that a fire will make it easy for him to find us," I told Dad.

Dad stroked his chin thoughtfully. "Well, if there is someone out there, I don't think it's going to be difficult for him to find us. It would be hard to lose fifty youth travelling at walking pace pushing handcarts. If someone is out there, he knows exactly where we are. He's probably biding his time. He might even be watching us right now."

I shivered, and it wasn't from the cold. "Thanks, Dad," I said sarcastically. "You're making me feel much better."

Dad saw the fear in my moon-washed face and knew that I was serious. "Look, I don't think we could convince two companies not to use a fire tonight. It's freezing at the moment, and I can't think up a believable excuse to stop them. But don't worry. I'll keep an eye out just in case there really is someone out there that wants to hurt us. I won't let anyone sneak up on us."

I found a smooth, flat piece of ground and spread my sleeping bag over it. A gust of cold wind sent a chill through me. "I hate the cold," I said, almost to myself. Things were already bad enough with that creep out in the bush somewhere, and the chill just added to the misery. With the assurance that Dad was watching over me, I closed my eyes and tried to get some sleep. But it was no use. The ground was too rough, and it was way too cold to sleep comfortably. To make matters worse, the image of the man staring at me kept on flashing through my mind. My imagination began to run wild as I imagined every worst possible scenario. I willed myself to stop thinking my morbid thoughts. I'm just tired, I told myself. Everything always seems scarier at night. I'll get some sleep, and everything will seem better in the morning. I used the corner of my rucksack as a pillow and tried to make myself as comfortable as I could. However my sleep was not restful. When I eventually drifted off to sleep, I had the most horrible nightmare.

I dreamt I was standing on an elevated platform. An unruly crowd had gathered around me, and all eyes were on me. My hands were tied behind my back and the rope was pulled so tight that it cut deep into my wrists. The crowd cheered and jeered and called out insults to me. Next to me stood a white-haired man in a dark pin-striped suit decorated with medals. "Do you have any final words?" the man asked me sneeringly.

"Why are you doing this to me?" I whimpered. "I don't deserve this. "

"Of course you deserve this," he snarled back. "You have been living off blood money your whole life. You have been enjoying the good things of life through what was taken from other people through crime and violence. You deserve everything that is happening to you, and I am ridding your crimes from this world."

"But I'm trying," I screamed. "I'm trying to change my life. That must count for something!""Not to me it doesn't," the man replied harshly. And with that he nodded to a thuggish executioner with massive arms and a huge thick neck. The executioner reached over and placed a noose around my neck. My heart began to beat faster as the executioner put his hand on the lever opening the trap door. I waited for the inevitable short drop that would cause my neck to snap and my spirit to leave my body. With a sudden jerk the executioner pulled down on the lever and I felt myself falling. . .

I woke up gasping. My heart was beating furiously, and I was covered with sweat. I took a deep breath and waited for my heart to stop thudding. I was too shaken by my dream to get back to sleep, but I knew that I would need all the energy that I could get for what was ahead of me. Being unable to sleep, I just lay awake and tried to get as much rest as I could. Finally, once the first rays of sun began to fill the sky, I slid out of my sleeping bag and stumbled out of the makeshift "tent" that we had created from the canvas that covered the handcart. The tent wasn't much, but at least it kept out the elements a little bit. As I got out, I saw that Dad was already awake and sitting on a log.

I was used to seeing Dad awake at unusual hours. Dad had always had trouble sleeping. It came with the life that he lived. But I knew that it wasn't insomnia keeping him up now. I figured that Dad must have stayed out there in the bitter cold all night keeping an eye out for the bloke that I had mentioned. I was touched that Dad would stay up all night to keep us safe. I didn't envy him walking all day after getting no sleep. I yawned and sat down next to Dad on the log.

There was something about the early morning hour and the closeness that I felt to Dad right then that made me feel like I could just speak to Dad about anything. "Dad," I asked him tentatively, "when did you first know that you wanted to change your life?"

Dad seemed to think for a moment. "It was when I visited our previous godfather in the hospital about five years ago," he told me. "He had been so powerful and strong. Everyone obeyed him without question, and he was respected and feared by everyone. But when I came down to the hospital to visit him, I was shocked by how frail and weak he looked. I realised that, despite all of his power, he was now going to leave this world empty-handed. The moment had come for him to face whatever is next, and

I could tell from the look in his eyes that he was afraid to die. He was unprepared to go into the next world. I realised that I didn't want to be like the godfather and reach the peak of power and success, only to die a frightened death".

I nodded. While I hoped that my own death was many, many years away, I often thought about the end of my life and what would happen next.

Dad sighed. "I have so many regrets," he told me sadly. "People think that a life in the mafia is a glamorous life. But they are so wrong. It is nothing like what you see in the movies. I thought that I was living the good life before, but now, for the first time ever, I feel like I love being alive."

Dad and I just talked until the sun rose over the horizon. Soon the sky was filed with red sunlight that just grew brighter and brighter and more dazzling. It was so nice to talk to Dad about things that really mattered under the sunrise.

My mind was still foggy with lack of sleep as I began to push the handcart that morning. I couldn't wait for trek to be over and to be able to once again sleep in my own bed. I so badly longed to laze around the house all day watching movies and eating as much junk food as I could. If I could just once again have my bed to sleep in, I would never complain about anything ever again.

"You know, that was the hardest thing for me on trek so far," Peter whispered to me as we pushed the handcart together. I had no idea what he was talking about. "What was?" I asked.

"The women's pull", Peter replied matter-of-factly.

"Yeah, right," I scoffed. "How was it hard for you? You just had to stand there and watch. It was the women that did all the work."

"That's exactly what made it the hardest part," Peter explained. "It was so difficult to just watch you pushing the handcart without being able to step in. I knew that the women's pull was going to happen, but I just hated not being able to help. It just broke my heart. I have so much respect for our young women now. And after seeing how hard you pushed yourself, I have so much respect for you, Chelsea."

I was touched by Peter's comments. The women's pull also filled me with awe and respect for our brave pioneer women who often did have to push handcarts without their husbands help. All too often, their husbands would have had to watch them from heaven pulling their handcarts all on their own.

The experience also made me reflect on the courage of other women in my life, particularly my mother. I thought about everything that she's done for me. I also realised that

I needed good men in my life: men like my father, and men like Peter. Everything seemed so much easier now that I had Peter back at my side once again pushing the handcart. One day I hoped to have a strong and worthy priesthood holder like Peter by my side forever.

After we struggled over a particularly difficult hill, we came across a clearing with a large, brightly coloured tepee. There were a number of big, muscular-looking men standing in front of the tepee. They were wearing breechcloths, blankets and fur caps ornamented with brightly coloured beads, and they all had serious expressions on their faces. I recognised them as some of the Polynesian members from our stake. Next to them stood a pretty young woman with raven black hair and dramatic brown eyes, who I recognised as Mele's older sister.

I looked over at Dad. "What do you think?" I asked. "Are they friendly or are they a threat to us?" Dad just shrugged. "Who knows?" he replied. "But I think we should trust them. And we are in need of food, so maybe they can give us some food."

As we approached, the group of Native Americans all looked towards a man with finer clothing than the others and red face paint. I figured he must be the chief. Dad approached this man respectfully. "Sir, we would like to ask your permission to pass through your land here. We have travelled a long distance, and we still have some way to go before we reach the land that the Great Spirit has prepared for us. May we please pass through your land?"

"You are welcome to pass through or to stay for a short time," the chief responded. "You will be safe on our land."

"Thank you," Dad acknowledged with a smile and a bow of his head. "Sir, we have used up almost all of our food for this journey, and we are greatly in need of food to sustain us for the rest of our journey. Do you have any food that we could buy or trade?"

"We are always happy to trade food," the chief told us kindly. "What do you have in exchange?" The chief took out a large bag and handed it to us. Dad opened it, and I peered in from over his shoulder. The bag was filled with bright, juicy oranges.

My mouth watered as I imagined biting into the sweetness of the oranges. I so wanted to make the trade. What did we have to give in exchange though? Dad rummaged through all of our belongings on the handcart. We had spare clothing, canvas, scriptures, rope, but we couldn't find anything that we didn't need for our journey. Then I thought of something. I reached behind my neck and took off the gold chain that Paul had given me. Dad frowned at first. "No, Chelsea," he told me gently. "I know that means a lot to you. And that gold chain is expensive. It is really one of the few expensive things that you still own."

"Dad, it's part of my old life," I replied. "In fact the last time I saw Paul, I was really afraid of him. Paul is no longer my friend, and I don't need it anymore. In any case, they'll probably just give it back to me once trek is over. It's all we have to trade. I'm happy to give it so our family can have some food."

Dad nodded, and I handed the chief my chain. The chief examined it closely but shook his head kindly. "We don't need you to give us your gold," he told me. "It is enough that you offered to give it to us. Please accept this food as a gift from us". With that the chief handed me the bag of oranges. I thanked him and began to hand out oranges to everyone. I took a big bite of my orange and savoured the taste. It tasted so sweet, so delicious. After what we had eaten the past number of days, I felt like I had never tasted anything so wonderful in my life "I never thought that I would feel so grateful for just an orange," I told Dad.

Dad smiled back at me. "I think that is one of the secrets to happiness—to take joy in the good, simple things of life." I leaned over and gave Dad a big hug. Yes, this is the good life, I thought. Just being here in the midst of nature with family and friends and enjoying the simple things of life. This was an adventure that I would always remember.

CHAPTER 15

"I don't like the look of those clouds," Dad muttered as he taped my shoes together. I had only walked for a few hours on the third day of trek when the sole came off from my right shoe. I wondered how I could possibly keep going with my shoes falling apart. However, the thought of me quitting never even crossed Dad's mind. He quickly pulled out his tape and began repairing my shoes. I stretched my arms and shoulders as Dad worked on fixing my shoe. I was aching all over from walking and pushing.

"I don't think I'd mind a little rain," Mum replied, rubbing the side of her neck, "just as long as it doesn't rain too heavily". I looked up at the sky. The clouds certainly were dark and looked pretty ominous.

"You should be able to manage like that," Dad told me once he had finished his taping job. It looked like he had almost used up the whole roll of tape. "C'mon, Dad," I protested. "I can't walk like this. This is just a big mess. My feet are now lopsided with all the extra layers that you've added." Dad, however, was clearly unconcerned. "Don't worry, Chelsea," he told me. "You'll be fine. We don't have too long to go."

As I continued to walk, my foot and knee began to throb, and I once again began to feel sorry for myself. "This really can't get any worse," I moaned. I kept on walking and pushing, thinking angry thoughts until I felt the Spirit gently chiding me for my whining. I realised that while wearing a taped-together shoe was uncomfortable, I still had so much to be grateful for. I thought about the pioneers who walked barefoot through the snow and ice until their feet were shredded. I thought of all those who lost toes and feet, fingers and hands to frostbite. Sure, it was cold here at night. But it wasn't that cold. And we all had shoes and gloves to protect us from the elements. All of a sudden I felt very grateful for shoes to walk in, even if they were held together by tape.

I was also wrong about things not been able to get any worse. As we continued along, I realised that the dark clouds I had noticed before had lowered over us. There was a rumble of thunder, followed by a flash of lightening, and within a moment it was raining cats and dogs. "Run," Dad yelled, and I saw that the whole company had dropped their handcarts and were scrambling for cover. The rain made damp weight of my dress, which was now blotched with mud and the rain. Dad slipped on the wet ground as he ran for cover. Trying to regain his balance, he fell hard onto his elbow and his knees.

"Yes!" I heard Brother Lawson cry out with delight. He was shading under a gum tree but was intently watching the chaos unfold. "I've been praying for this."

Something just snapped when I heard Brother Lawson's remark. I was tired and sore and shivering from the cold, bone-chilling rain, and all of a sudden I saw red. I stormed up to Brother Lawson furiously. Great big drops of water fell from my hair and clothes onto the ground as I rushed over to him, and I was still breathing heavily when I reached him. Brother Lawson was just as soaked as the rest of us. His clothing was plastered to his body, and his thinning, grey hair was slicked down by the rain. "You're so mean!" I spat at him. "Only you would want this to be a miserable experience for us."

I thought that Brother Lawson didn't have the capacity for any emotions except for bitterness and anger, but all of a sudden he looked really hurt and deflated. "Chelsea, you don't understand," he told me gently, his voice only barely audible over the sound of the wind and the rain. "I want trek to be difficult and to stretch you. I want you to know that you have unlimited potential and that you can do hard things. I want this to be so tough that you remember and talk about trek for the rest of our life. That is why I have been praying for this to be hard for you."

I didn't know how to respond to that, so I slowly turned and returned to my family. We huddled under a tree and waited out the worst part of the storm. When it was clear that it was going to continue to rain for the foreseeable future, we once again took our place on the handcarts and resumed the push. It was so disheartening pushing the handcart through the mud while being pattered by a thousand raindrops. I lowered my head against the onrushing wind and rain and daydreamed about how much I would enjoy my warm, dry bed once this was all over. After what seemed like an eternity, the rain slowed to a drizzle. I was still soaked, and I shivered constantly while we continued to push.

As I cast my eyes into the shrubbery, I saw something that made my blood run cold. I thought I saw a set of eyes in the midst of the bushes. A set of eyes staring right at me. My heart was beating furiously in my chest now. However, when I looked again, I couldn't see anything. Had I imagined it? Evening was approaching, and perhaps the fading light was playing tricks on me. And yet I didn't think so. I clearly saw a set of eyes staring right at me. The hair stood up on the back of my neck as the image of those eyes flashed through my mind again. There was something sinister about those eyes. And even though I could no longer see them, I couldn't shake the sickly feeling that those eyes were still watching me somewhere.

Who was this person that was watching me? I wondered. Was it the same person that I saw before? I really couldn't tell as I hadn't seen anything more than the eyes. However, there was something that I was certain about. The person might be out of my sight, but I was sure that I wasn't out of his or her sight.

CHAPTER 16

I tried to convince myself that I must have imagined the person. Or that it was one of the support crew who was trying to stay hidden behind the scenes. But I didn't really believe it. It seemed like too much of a coincidence in light of the other bloke that I had caught staring at me. And I was now really worried. Catching one person staring at me in the middle of the bush was strange, but to catch a second person was completely chilling. I tried to push the frightening thought out of my mind and to think of happier things.

We continued to pull the handcart through the drizzle until we reached a clearing. As we approached the clearing, I was surprised to see a bearded man on a magnificent black stallion. The man was rough looking, but there was a certain innocence and purity about him. The stallion neighed, and his nostrils flared. He shook his mane as he saw us approach.

The man smiled at us and greeted us warmly. "I've been looking for you," he told us kindly. "And I am very glad that I have now found you. My name is Ephraim Hanks, and I'm here to help you." We all looked at each other uncertainly. The name Ephraim Hanks sounded familiar to me, although I couldn't remember who he was in pioneer history.

Ephraim held out a sack for us and motioned for us to come forward. "Why don't you collect it for us," Mum told Bridget. Bridget edged forward and gratefully accepted the sack from Ephraim and brought it back to us. We gathered around and peered in as Bridget opened it. It seemed to be filled with beef jerky.

"Its buffalo meat," Ephraim explained. "Although buffalos are extremely scarce at this time of year, the Lord put buffalo in my path. I know that when we need something, the Lord is there for us."

The beef jerky tasted great. And it really did give me the strength I needed to keep going. By this point, I was exhausted and felt like giving up. Furthermore, I was feeling pretty unnerved after seeing those sinister eyes in the bush.

I couldn't shake the feeling that someone with evil intentions was watching me. But I began to feel a little better as I ate the beef jerky. I felt more solid, and the strength began to return to my muscles. Thank goodness we only had one more day to go before trek would be over. I imagined that everyone felt the same way. Bridget, Carly, Nancy and Steve were all also looking pretty worn out. Only Peter looked as if the strenuous past few days had barely fazed him. Peter looked like he could keep going for another four days.

We were all sitting on the ground munching on our beef jerky when I saw Brother Lawson approach our group. I tensed up, wondering if he was going to tell us off for something that we had done wrong, but his manner seemed more relaxed and more pleasant than I ever recall seeing before. He even seemed happy. Although he spoke to the whole group, he kept on making eye contact with me and at one stage even gave me a warm smile. "We have a surprise for you all today!" he said excitedly. "We're going to have a dance tonight."

"A dance?" I asked, giving him an quizzical look. "Out here? That's not very pioneer-like, is it?"

"Oh, it's not the kind of dance that you're thinking of, Chelsea," Brother Lawson replied, and he actually laughed. "There will be no Beyonce, no Pentatonix. It will be nineteenth-century line dancing."

Brother Lawson organised the company into teams to prepare for the dance. We had to have everything prepared by the time it got dark, and there was a lot of work to do. However, the promise of a dance lifted everyone's spirits, and we all worked with a renewal of energy in the fading light. I did wonder how good a dance in the middle of the bush would really be, but it turned out to be an amazing experience. There was something magical about having a dance that was lit by a bonfire. Having real flames created an atmosphere of warmth and cosiness that I had never experienced at any other dance.

The dance, however, wasn't completely historically authentic. We didn't have people playing fiddles or anything like that. Sister Mahanga had set up speakers in a tent next to the clearing, and she played various nineteenth-century waltzes throughout the night. And yet, it all felt real enough. Trek had been so intense that I think that we all needed to let off a little steam and have some fun.

The dance was pretty subdued to begin with. We weren't used to dancing to nineteenth-century music. And we were all pretty fatigued. Often you don't realise how tired you are until you stop and rest for a while. Now that we finally had a change to relax, exhaustion was beginning to set in for a lot of us. But as the night wore on, the youth slowly began to let loose. The dance was an escape and a stress release for a lot of people, and soon the night was filled with fun and roars of laughter.

Luckily tonight wasn't as cold as the previous nights had been, and with the bonfire and all the activity, everyone managed to stay warm enough. I was the only person at the dance who was feeling the cold. Everyone else was dancing and having the time of their lives, but joining in was not an option for me. Walking with shoes that had been sticky-taped together had really done my feet in, and my feet were now so swollen that it hurt to even wear shoes, let alone dance in them. I looked across the dance floor and saw that Peter was dancing with Carly as his partner. Carly looked very happy to have Peter all to herself. Peter was cordial and friendly, but I could tell from his body language that he didn't have the same feelings for Carly as she had for him. His dancing was a little standoffish, and while Carly kept on wanting to cling to Peter, Peter kept on moving back.

As I sat on the log, watching the youth swirl around me and have a great time, I began to feel really awkward. Everyone was having fun except for me. Everyone was staying warm and being active and building memories except me. I had at first been content watching everyone else, but I now began to feel as if I was missing out. I was tired of being a spectator instead of a participant. I cursed my swollen feet and wished that I was well enough to participate fully in the dance. Time just stretched on, and as it passed, my frustration intensified. After what seemed like an eternity, Peter forced his way through the crowd towards me. My heart skipped a beat when I saw him coming. He is so good-looking, I thought to myself. I smiled up at Peter as he stood in front of me. I was glad he had come over. I was lonely and in need of a friend right now.

"May I have this dance?" Peter asked me with a bow. I had already told Peter earlier on that I would be sitting this dance out, but I guess he wanted to at least ask me anyway. I just shook my head sadly. "You know I'd love to, Peter, but my feet are just so sore". Peter looked like he was going to say something further when a pretty girl with wavy, blond hair and soulful blue eyes came over and looped her arm through Peter's. "Peter, come and dance with me," she purred at him. Peter flashed me a final smile before he was led away.

I kicked myself as soon as Peter was out of sight. I have this one chance to dance with Peter underneath the silvery moonlight and the stars and next to the bonfire. And I've just let the opportunity slip by, simply because my feet are sore. And yet I had managed to push my handcart for many hours earlier today. I thought about what both Dad and Brother Lawson had said about building memories on trek and wanted this dance to be a special memory, not a memory that I regretted.

After that dance was over, I pushed my way through the crowd towards Peter. He held out his hand for me when he saw me coming. "I'm so glad that you decided to dance with me after all," he told me happily. I smiled back at him. As I took his hand, my heart began to beat with excitement. I forgot about my aching feet as we danced together.

Not everyone was happy, however, that I had changed my mind about dancing. As I glanced across the dance ground, I saw Carly staring at me, her face a mask of rage. She looked like she wanted to hurt me. I turned my back on her as I danced, but I continued to feel her eyes boring into the back of my head. Once that dance was over, Carly stormed away, disappearing into the darkness.

As I glanced around, I noticed that Mum and Dad were also nowhere in sight. They were meant to be chaperoning us, and I couldn't imagine them ditching the dance. I motioned to Bridget, who was dancing with Steve, to come over. "Have you seen Mum and Dad?" I asked her once she had made her way across the dance ground. "They should be here."

"No, afraid not," Bridget replied with a puzzled look on her face. "You know, I was wondering about that myself.

Maybe they just decided to have an early night. Your mum was looking pretty exhausted before!"

I hoped that that was the case, but I was worried all the same. Once Bridget returned to dancing, I told Peter that I was going to return to the camp and see if Mum and Dad were there. "Is everything okay?" he asked me. "Do you want me to come with you?"

"No, everything is fine," I told him. "I just want to check up on Mum and Dad. I think I'm done dancing anyway. You stay here and enjoy the dance. It wouldn't look good for us to be seen sneaking away from the dance together in any case."

I began to limp to camp, peering through the darkness. My feet were still giving me grief, but I figured that I'd rest them once I found Mum and Dad. The further I hobbled away from the dance, the darker it got. Soon I found myself immersed in darkness. While a little bit of moonlight filtered down through the trees, the bush felt dark and hostile and deserted, and all of a sudden I felt incredibly vulnerable. I now regretted not getting someone to come with me. Even if I didn't want to give people the wrong impression by leaving the dance with Peter, I could at least have taken Bridget with me instead.

For a while I felt my way along with my hands, making sure that I didn't walk into any sharp branches. However, my eyes soon began to adjust to the dim light, and I was then able to walk around more freely.

Everything was deadly quiet at first, and all that I could hear was the crunch of my own feet on the leafy ground. However, I soon began to hear strange noises all around me in the bushland. A sharp wind began to howl around me, causing the branches of the gum trees to creak. My heart began beating quickly when I heard a rustling in the bushes just behind me. I quickly spun around, but I couldn't see anything.

Now I was worried. Where was the camp? I felt so vulnerable, so alone. My heart began beating faster as I realised that if something happened to me here, no one would even know where I was.

Suddenly the hairs stood up on the back of my neck as I heard a rustling in the bushes in front of me. I held my breath as I squinted into the darkness at the bushes. "Who—who's there?" I stammered, my throat tightening. But there was no reply. I realised that my heart was pounding and that I was breathing heavily. My eyes darted around the bush to see if there was anyone there that I could call on for help. But there was no one. No one would even hear me scream

I nearly jumped out of my skin when a large, shadowy figure jumped right out in front of me. My worst fears were coming true. I was being attacked with no one there to save me. I opened my mouth and screamed.

CHAPTER 17

I stared ahead and saw a large kangaroo bouncing off into the darkness. I think I scared the kangaroo just as much as it scared me. I breathed a sigh of relief and tried to force my breathing to return to normal. I still felt all jittery, and so I leaned against a tree while I waited for my pulse to slow.

As I continued to stagger my way towards camp, the wind howled around me, and the trees shook in the wind. I was still on edge. I kept alert, peering into the blackness, but I couldn't see anything. The bush was so dark, and everything was eerily quiet. I felt overwhelmed by a sense of my own vulnerability and insignificance.

As I continued to limp along, a man stepped out of the shadows and stepped menacingly towards me. He was tall and rough looking with a long, straggly beard. I let out a startled gasp and took a few steps back. He was pretty scary looking. "Where do you think you're going, Chelsea?" he demanded. Goosebumps rose up my neck, but my muscles relaxed once I realised that he looked familiar to me. He was dressed in nineteenth-century clothing, and so I figured that he must be in the support crew and in costume as a mob member. I smiled. Let's hope that this one doesn't trip on something and bowl me over.

All of a sudden a feeling of dread swept over me as I recognised the man. I realised that I was wrong, and another mob attack was the least of our concerns. I shuddered as I realised that it wasn't church that I recognised him from.

Before I could do anything, he pulled out a shiny object and pointed it at my chest. I saw the gleam of metal in the moonlight. As my eyes focused on the object, I saw that it was a pistol. Yes, he was a member of the mob all right, I thought. Just not the mob that I had been thinking of. I hadn't recognised him in the dark and with his beard. But now there was no mistake. It was Carlos. He stared at me with an evil look in my eye. "It took a long time," Carlos hissed. "But we finally caught you. Now tonight, you and your family are going to die."

CHAPTER 18

I opened my mouth, ready to scream. But my scream caught in my throat as Carlos cocked his pistol. "I wouldn't," he told me menacingly.

This is it, I thought. They've finally caught up with us, and I am as good as dead. Had they caught up with Mum and Dad already? I wondered. I shuddered, and tears came to my eyes as the thought forced its way into my mind— could Mum and Dad be dead already? I forced the thought out of my mind.

"Where's my mother and father?" I demanded, aiming for a bravado I did not really feel. "What have you done with them? If you've hurt them in any way, you'll be sorry."

Carlos laughed a cold, hard laugh. "I'd be more worried about yourself if I were you. But don't worry. You'll see them soon enough." Carlos motioned with his pistol, and I began walking in front of him in the direction that he had indicated.

After walking for what seemed like forever, we eventually arrived at a clearing. As we approached, I saw a large man digging a deep hole in the ground. As the moonlight filtered down through the treetops, I realised that it was Dad. I felt a flood of relief and offered a silent prayer of thanks that Dad was okay. My eyes darted around the clearing looking for Mum, but I couldn't see her anywhere. I saw a flash of blond hair in the moonlight. As I focused in on the figure, I saw that it belonged to a man with huge brawny shoulders and a broad neck. He was keeping a watchful eye on Dad, and he was even bigger than my father. In fact Dad barely came up to his shoulders. He looked like he must have been at least six foot five, I thought with alarm. He looked like he worked out at the gym. A lot.

The man glared at Dad with pure hatred as Dad dug, and he looked like he could easily reach over and snap Dad in half. Not that he would even need to lay a hand on Dad. He had a pistol pointed straight at Dad's head, and so he would be able to extinguish Dad's life at will with a squeeze of a trigger. Standing next to the hulk was another large man with a goatee, solid arms and an open shirt. I recognised him as the man I had caught watching me on that first occasion.

I continued to dart my eyes in all directions, frantically looking for Mum. I eventually found her on a log at the edge of the clearing. Mum was tugging and straining at a rope which bound her wrists together. Her mouth was gagged, she was blindfolded, and she was sobbing and trembling uncontrollably. "Mum! Dad!" I screamed out, my voice breaking. "Chelsea!" Mum called back in a muffled, distorted voice. She sounded almost hysterical as she screamed through her gag.

Dad turned in my direction, and a look of anguish crossed his face when he saw me being led at gunpoint. The hulk gave Dad a shove and gestured to him to keep digging. Dad turned to him pleadingly. "Look, Charles,

I'm the only one that knows your dirty little secrets," Dad begged. "Once you kill me, you're safe. Just leave my wife and daughter alone."

But Charles just sneered. "You know the way this works, John," he replied coolly. Dad suddenly exploded with rage. "Do what you want with me!" Dad roared. "But I swear that if you try to touch my wife or daughter, I will kill you!" Charles lashed out so quickly I barely saw it, striking Dad brutally across the face with the handle of his pistol. Dad uttered a startled groan, his eyes bulging in pain before he fell to his knees. As Dad's knees buckled, Charles let out an angry growl and launched a vicious kick at Dad's stomach. "Noooo!" I screamed as his foot landed with sickening force deep into Dad's stomach, sending him hurtling backwards into the dirt.

Dad struggled to get up. He pulled himself to his hands and knees, coughing and spluttering and gasping for air. He raised himself to one knee, his other hand still clutching his stomach. "You're in no position to make threats," Charles told Dad drily. "Now keep digging. Or else I'll shoot them right now." The man with the goatee then walked over to Mum, who was sobbing away, and held his pistol next to her head. Dad groggily got to his feet and obediently continued digging.

It was just too much for me to see Mum and Dad treated in this way. I felt sick to my stomach, and couldn't just stand there doing nothing. I made a dash to run to Mum, but Carlos ran after me and grabbed me roughly by the arm. I struggled with all of my strength to break free from his grip, but it was no use. Carlos was much stronger than I was. I grunted with exertion and thrashed about, but he held me tightly, almost effortlessly, with just one arm while he kept the pistol pointed at me with the other.

"Let me go!" I shrieked. "Let my parents go!" But Carlos didn't answer me. Instead he threw me against a tree, knocking all the breath out of my lungs. I was stunned, and dizziness swept over me. I gasped for air while the man with the goatee took a rope and tied me tightly against the tree. I strained and struggled with all my strength, and pain shot up my arms as the ropes cut deeper into my flesh.

Carlos stepped in front of me, his cold, hard face inches away from mine. I had always been afraid of Carlos, but in the darkness he appeared more terrifying than ever. My eyes opened wide with horror as Carlos reached into his pocket and pulled out a switchblade. His face gleamed with hatred as he flicked the knife open, the blade glimmering in the moonlight. "What are you doing?!" I shrieked at him. The fright gave me the energy to once again strain against the ropes, but the more I struggled, the more they cut into me.

He sneered at me. "I'll wait for your Dad to finish. And then we are going to kill all three of you."

Of course I knew that this was their plan, but a shiver of fear ran down my back to hear Carlos explain it so bluntly, so matter-of-factly. There was no escaping it. The time for them to kill us had finally arrived. I felt sick with fear, but a phrase from the hymn "Come, Come, Ye Saints" flashed suddenly through my mind: "Fresh courage take. . ." I decided that if the pioneers could die with the courage that they showed, then I could too. "Mum, Dad, it's alright," I called out. "If I die with you, so be it. All that matters is that we stick together as a family. If we do die, at least we all die together!"

Mum stopped sobbing as she heard my words. She was blindfolded and couldn't see me, but she looked in the direction of my voice. Dad paused his digging for the moment. "That's my brave girl," Dad told me proudly. Charles gave Dad a rough shove, and Dad continued his digging. Choking back tears, I did the only thing left that I could do. I prayed for my family and myself. I sent up to heaven heartfelt pleading for all of us. I prayed that our loving and kind Heavenly Father would save our lives. But if it wasn't His will for our lives to be spared, I prayed that he would at least give us a sense of peace and that He would be with us in our final moments. But with all my pleading, I also sent up prayers of gratitude. I thanked Heavenly Father for my family, for the gospel, and that we were together at this time. I thanked him that we would die together, unified, and for the knowledge that we could be together forever as a family. I kept on praying until Carlos decided that the holes were deep enough. "Okay, that will do," he said, nodding to Charles. "Time to fill them."

I looked over and saw that Dad had finished digging three graves. And they were the perfect size for the three of us.

CHAPTER 19

Charles pointed his pistol straight at Dad's head. "Kneel!" he ordered, and I watched in horror as Dad resignedly got down on his knees. Frozen with horror, I watched as Charles placed the pistol to the back of Dad's head. My stomach turned as Charles then shot a glance in my direction and smiled at me. It was such a cruel and taunting smile. He's evil, I realised. There was no mercy or compassion in his expression. He was enjoying our fear and toying with us. There was no doubt about it; he was going to kill us all, and he was going to enjoy it.

I tried to reason with the man with the goatee. "Don't let him do this," I pleaded, my voice cracking. "This is murder! You have got to stop him." But he completely ignored me. He acted like he hadn't even heard me.

There was only one thing left to try. I opened my mouth to scream for help. I screamed at the top of my lungs, my throat aching with the intensity. It worked for the moment. Charles lowered his pistol and turned in my direction, distracted by my screaming. All of a sudden Carlos slugged me with a massive right hook that snapped my head back. My head was crushed between the impact of Carlos' punch and the back of the tree trunk. Blood trickled down from the corner of my mouth and dripped onto the front of my dress. Everything began to go dark, but I struggled to maintain consciousness. I couldn't afford to allow myself to black out. I needed my wits to work a way out of this.

My head was now throbbing with pain. I wasn't going to scream again. All that was left was to plead for our lives. "Please!" I choked out, tears streaming down my face, "Don't kill us. Let us live." But it was no use. Carlos, like his henchman, was incapable of pity. He just stood there coldly as Charles, momentarily distracted by my scream, once again placed his pistol to the back of Dad's head.

By now I was more terrified than I had ever been before in my life. My heart was pounding away in my chest. "Dad!!!" I screamed, and Dad looked over at me and smiled gently. I braced myself for the worst and looked away.

But the dreaded gunshot never came. Instead I heard a deep, authoritative voice say "No one is to harm them." I exhaled deeply, and relief flooded my body. As I focused in the dark, I saw Bruce Moretti, our godfather, step out of the shadows. Paul was right by his side, and he was being followed by three other stocky men in slacks and brightly coloured shirts. Carlos's jaw dropped open when he saw our godfather. While I was extremely grateful for this intervention, it did occur to me that we might be out of the frying pan but into the fire. "Get out of here," the godfather told Carlos and his men. Carlos looked like he was about to protest, but he stopped short when Paul reached into his jacket. Carlos and his goons scurried off as quickly as they could and without another word.

Once Carlos and his men had left, our godfather looked down on my bruised and beaten father. Dad's eye was almost swollen shut, and the front of his shirt was stained with blood. "Did you really think I wouldn't be able to find you, John?" our godfather chided. "I thought that you knew me better than that. You know that I am always two steps ahead of everyone else. That's how I got to where I am. That's why I'm still alive while so many of my friends are dead. I'm disappointed that you underestimated me in this way."

"I didn't underestimate you, Godfather," Dad replied respectfully. "I guess I always knew that this day would come when you would catch up with me. I only ask that you be merciful and spare my family. I hope you understand why I did what I did. I had to try and change my life and try to right my wrongs."

I tried to read our godfather's reaction, but he was difficult to read. My mouth went dry as our godfather folded his arms and glanced at Paul. The godfather's eyebrows came together in a frown, and I swallowed. Dad clearly couldn't handle the suspense any longer either. He looked up at the godfather with resignation. "So what are you going to do to me now, Godfather? Are you going to kill me?" he asked.

"John, I've known you for a long time," the godfather replied, and we all hung on every word. "I've known you since you were a young boy," he continued, "and I've loved you as if you were my own son. But despite my love for you, I wouldn't hesitate to kill you and your family if you double-crossed me. Just like I've killed so many others who have double-crossed me."

I held my breath. I think we all did. The godfather motioned to Paul, and I stared at Paul in horror as he flicked open a switchblade and stepped menacingly towards me. I swallowed hard, my eyes locked on the knife. I was terrified now. My heart began beating furiously, and a wave of fear forced its way down my spine. I couldn't believe I was back in this situation after all that. For just a moment, I thought that I had been rescued, and it was crushing to realise after all that that this was not the case.

And the betrayal just added to the pain. I couldn't believe that Paul would be the person that would end up killing me. I knew he was angry with me, but we had shared a lot of good times as well. I had once loved him. It hurt so much that Paul was willing to kill me just like that at the godfather's command.

I didn't want to die. I was way too young and had so much more that I needed to do with my life. And yet I was helpless to do anything except await my impending death. I whimpered as Paul brought the blade towards me. And I braced myself for the agony of death.

CHAPTER 20

I had heard people say that your life flashes before your eyes at a moment of impending death, and that is exactly what I experienced. The film that played before my eyes, however, had been heavily edited. I remembered my happy, innocent moments as a child. However, the film skipped past my teenage years of pride, corruption and immorality as if they had never occurred. I went straight from my innocent, childhood days to seeing myself being taught by Sisters Green and Latu and being baptised together with Mum and Dad. And right then I knew that God had accepted my repentance and had forgotten my wayward teenage years. Despite all of my mistakes and regrets, I knew that my life was now right with God. I could die with a clear conscience, and this knowledge gave me the greatest satisfaction that I had ever experienced. I may be about to die, but my death would not be bitter to me.

Again the words of "Come, Come Ye Saints" came to my mind:

And should we die before our journey's through,
Happy day! All is well!
We then are free from toil and sorrow, too;
With the just we shall dwell!

Right then and there, I understood that line like I never had before. I so badly wanted to live to complete my trek. But if I died before my journey was through, I knew that I would be with God and that all would be well. I felt it in my heart and in my bones.

My heart was in my throat as Paul stepped in close to me and lowered his blade. The colour drained from my face, and tears began to trickle down my cheeks. I once again struggled to break free from my bonds, but it was no use. I braced myself and held my breath. Paul reached down and began to saw through the ropes that bound me to the tree. Paul saw the look of surprise on my face and looked hurt for a moment. "You didn't think I was going to harm you, did you?" he asked. "Chelsea, I would never do anything to you. When I heard that Carlos was after your family, I approached the godfather and asked him to step in on your behalf. You and your family have more friends than you know."

Paul then stepped away from me and towards Dad. He flashed Dad a knowing smile before pulling Dad to his feet. Dad and Paul rushed up to Mum, and together they quickly freed her from her bonds. While Dad still appeared cool and collected on the outside, I could see that his hands were trembling as he pulled Mum's ropes free. Even after Dad had pulled off her blindfold and gag, Mum just sat there sobbing uncontrollably and shaking from head to foot. "I almost just lost my whole family," she sobbed as Dad held her tight.

The godfather watched the unfolding scene before continuing. He had such an imposing presence, and everyone fell silent and turned to him as soon as he began talking. "But John, you didn't double-cross me," he told Dad kindly. "You just sought a better life. And I can respect that."

I was stunned. The godfather was showing us mercy. He was even speaking to Dad kindly. This was a side to the godfather that I had never seen, and I was flabbergasted. The godfather must have really respected Dad to make such a concession for him. And I knew that Paul had taken a big risk in asking the godfather to step in on our behalf. In essence, Paul had now sold his soul to the godfather. He owed the godfather, and the godfather would certainly collect in due time. How I wished that Paul could also have escaped the mafia life with us. By saving our lives, he had paved the way for his further corruption. But he had definitely proven himself to be a true friend.

As if reading my thoughts, the godfather continued. "It is true that I have shown you mercy today. But don't get me wrong and mistake this mercy for weakness. John, you know secrets that you need to take to your grave. If you don't, you and your family will all disappear." He said this so nonchalantly, so matter-of-factly. Making us disappear would just be a normal course of business for him, and that realisation sent shivers down my spine. "But if you can keep your secrets," the godfather promised, "I swear that you'll never have anything to fear from a member of the family."

When Dad replied, his voice was heavy with relief. "Godfather, we are all so grateful," Dad told him. "But I still don't understand why you saved us. I really thought that you were going to kill all of us. Or at least let Carlos kill us"

The godfather sighed. "I am saving you because you've managed to do what I've always wanted to do," he told us in a weary voice. "You've left the mafia and turned your life around and have become a good man. Not only can I respect that, but I envy that as well. There are so many times that I have wished that I could leave this life and become a good man too."

Dad thought about that for a moment. "You know you could join us, Godfather," Dad told him earnestly. "You could change. You could become a good man too."

But the godfather simply shook his head. "No, it's too late for me," he replied with resignation. "I know that I'll be damned for what I do. But this is the life I chose. I cannot unchoose it. But if you can, good on you."

With that the godfather motioned to Paul and the others. They then turned and walked away. Within a moment they had all disappeared into the darkness. Mum, Dad and I just stood there in silence, overcome by what had just happened. We didn't even dare to talk. We wanted to make sure that we really were safe and that there really wasn't anyone who was going to come back for us and hurt us. As I sat down on a log, I noticed that my entire body was still shaking. I took in deep breaths, trying to calm myself, while Dad draped his arm over my shoulder.

Dad motioned for Mum to come in so that he had his arms wrapped around both of us. "Never forget," he said solemnly, his voice lowering to a whisper, "what God has done for us this day. We chose a new life as a family, and He has kept us safe so that we can pursue that life. With the Godfather's protection, we never need to look over our shoulder again. I never need to go to bed wondering whether I'll live to see the sunrise. God has given us this gift, but how we live the rest of our lives can be our gift to God."

CHAPTER 21

With his arm still around our shoulders, Dad led us. "I'm so sorry that you both had to go through that," he whispered into our ears. "You've been through so much. Let's get you back to camp so that you can get some rest."

The dance had long since closed, and the camp was deadly quite. Dad checked on our trek family, but they were all already asleep. I was still trembling, and so Dad lit a fire and boiled a hot chocolate for me. "It's okay, Chelsea," Mum told me soothingly as she placed the hot chocolate in my hand. "It's all over now. " I took a sip of my drink, letting the rich chocolate warm me, and I slowly stopped shaking. Once I had finished my cup I just stared into nothingness.

Eventually I decided to get some rest and climbed into my sleeping bag. I didn't think that I would be able to sleep after such an emotional night. How does one sleep after almost being murdered? But once I was in my sleeping bag, I did feel a sense of comfort. All wrapped up, and in the calm and peace of the bush, I felt as if all the horrors of the night were shut out and forgotten. I offered an exhausted prayer of thanks to God for saving our lives, and within moments of closing my eyes I fell into peaceful oblivion.

I stirred from my sleep as the sun began to rise. I wanted to see Mum and Dad before the rest of our trek family joined us. I knew that what we had suffered the previous night was our secret to keep. We couldn't tell anyone about it or talk about it once the others joined us. None of them would really understand anyway. And so the only thing to do when the others joined us was to pretend that nothing was wrong.

Mum and Dad were alone, warming themselves by the fire. Dad's face looked even worse in the early morning light than it had last night. He had an ugly purple welt under his eye, and underneath that, Dad's face was swollen and blue.

"How's your head?" I asked Dad as I gently touched his eye with my fingertips. Dad just shrugged. "I'll live," he told me casually. I tenderly touched my jaw. It was still sore, but at least I didn't look as beat up as Dad. I poured some water from my bottle onto a handkerchief and dabbed at the bloodstains on the front of my dress. Luckily it was a purple dress, and the blood didn't show up very clearly. Thankfully trek was almost over. I just needed to avoid any questions about last night for the remainder of the journey, and then we would be home clear. I sat in between Mum and Dad, and we watched as the red sunrise grew brighter and brighter. It grew more radiant, more beautiful, more dazzling with each passing minute, and it filled me with a sense of elation that we had survived the night.

The rest of the family stared at Dad's face as they arose and joined us at the campfire. They were clearly waiting for some kind of explanation about why Dad's face was a mess. However, Dad just ignored their quizzical looks and acted as if nothing had happened.

I was feeling very emotional when I took my place at the front to push the handcart the next morning. Peter looked over at me curiously. "Hey, where did you and your parents disappear to last night?" he asked. "And what time did you all come to bed?"

"Oh, not too late," I told him. "We just had a bit of a family issue."

"Oh," Peter replied, looking confused. "Hey, what happened to your Dad's face?"

"Oh, you know my dad," I explained. "He's a bit of a klutz. He couldn't see where he was going in the dark and ended up rolling down a hill. He's a bit bruised, but he'll be okay."

"Well, I'm glad that he's okay. He looks like he was tortured by a bunch of mobsters."

I faked an awkward laugh and tried to change the subject. "Was everyone okay while we were gone?" I asked. Peter nodded. "Yeah, I took charge of the family after you disappeared. I organised a family prayer and then got everyone off to bed."

"That's good," I told him. "I'm sure Mum and Dad will appreciate that."

"Is everything really okay with your family?" Peter asked me kindly. "Is there anything I can help with?"

"Thanks, but don't worry about us," I told him. "We're all going to be fine from now on."

It was the final day of trek and so the end was in sight. I tried to lose myself in the journey so that I wouldn't have to think. It was such a difficult day for me, and it took all of my mental and physical strength to keep pushing. I was emotionally drained, and my feet were now so swollen that I could barely wear my shoes. But I was grateful for the pain. It distracted me from my thoughts and allowed me to focus on something else. We ended up walking longer that day than we had on any other day of trek, and the day passed for me in a daze.

"So what are you going to do when you get home?" Peter asked me during our lunch break. We were eating cheese and ham sandwiches, which were the most substantial meal we had had on trek so far. I think that they were spoiling us now that trek was almost over.

"I think that the first thing I'm going to do is take a long, hot shower," I told him wistfully. "I'll wash my hair and stay in until we run out of hot water. And then I'll put on some clean pyjamas and sleep in a warm bed with clean sheets. I'll probably sleep for two days straight." I couldn't stop smiling as I pictured myself under the quilt of my cosy, warm bed. Right there and then, it seemed like the best thing in the world.

"What about you?" I asked Peter. I thought that he would likewise be craving a shower or warm bed or perhaps a hot meal. However, it seemed that Peter had been suffering withdrawals of another kind. "I think that the first thing that I'll do is hop on to the Xbox," he told me.

"What, you mean even before you have a shower or change your clothes?" I asked, rolling my eyes.

"Yeah, if my mum will let me."

"I doubt that she will," I told him bluntly. "You really stink. Don't take it the wrong way; we all do. But I think you better take a shower as soon as you get home."

After lunch Brother Wilder, our trail boss, announced that we would be having a testimony meeting. We all sat in a circle as the youth one by one shared their testimonies. There were no awkward pauses the way there sometimes were in fast and testimony meetings. The youth were hungry, eager to share the wonderful spiritual experiences that they had had on trek. I loved the meeting, and I felt the Spirit so powerfully as I listened to all the testimonies. Bridget, Peter and Steve each got up and shared their testimonies about how they had grown closer to God on trek and how grateful they were for the experience. This didn't really surprise me. They were all very spiritual to begin with, and I could see them stretch and grow during trek. I was very surprised, however, when Nancy got up to bear her testimony.

Nancy slowly stood up and glared at her audience. She took a deep breath before beginning. Her hands were shaking. She was obviously nervous about speaking in front of everyone. Nancy had clearly not been enjoying her Spartan trek adventure, and I worried about what she was about to say. I hoped that she wouldn't bring down this really spiritual testimony meeting with her complaints and whinging.

"You know, I wasn't brought up in the church," Nancy began, "and so I never got the opportunity to go on trek as a youth. And I was fine with that. I knew that trek was going to be really hard, and I was glad to be in the support crew where we would be warmer, have better food, and most of all, not have to push handcarts. And then Steve practically forced me to join his family." And with these words Nancy began glaring at Steve.

Uh-oh, here it comes, I thought. I waited for Nancy to unleash a torrent of abuse at Steve for what he had put her through. But the words that came out of her mouth next were not what I was expecting.

"Steve, thank you so much for bringing me into your family," Nancy blurted out with tears in her eyes. "All these years, I didn't know what I was missing. It's been a life-changing experience for me. I've learnt that I can do hard things. I've learnt that God really is there and that He cares about my life. I'm so grateful to you and your family for taking me in. Even though I constantly complained, you made me feel like I was part of your family." And with that, Nancy walked over and gave Steve a big hug. Steve was taken aback and turned red with embarrassment. I knew that Steve was shy and didn't like the attention. All the same, Steve had a big smile plastered on to his face for the rest of the afternoon.

The sun blazed down on us from the clear, blue sky as we once again began pushing the handcart. I knew that we were on the home run now. I looked around at our family and noticed how tired everyone looked. Mum and Dad were both very sunburnt, and Mum's nose was beginning to peel. Bridget had deep shadows under her eyes, and Carly, Nancy and Steve all looked like they could do with a good night's sleep. Peter was still the only one that looked fresh.

As we continued to push, I began to hear some of the most beautiful singing that I had ever heard. Marian Lopez and Allison Travers from the Semmler family had begun singing "Come, Come Ye Saints." Both girls were extremely talented and often performed in public. And right then and there, they both sounded like angels. Others began to join in, and before I knew it, we were all singing. We weren't all as talented as Marian and Allison, but that didn't matter. Together we sounded amazing, and I felt goosebumps as I sang with my fellow youth. I felt unified with them all. Everyone was sunburnt and worn. Our clothes were dusty, and our faces were streaked with dirt. Some of the youth looked like they were about to collapse. And through our pain and suffering we had developed a sense of brotherhood and sisterhood. We had grown closer together by overcoming together.

I could tell that we were beginning to approach civilisation. Fences began to appear, and we saw paddocks full of sheep and horses as we pushed. Suddenly Bridget started pointing. Another old church materialized on the horizon, and I could see that there was a large crowd of people surrounding it. As I got closer, I recognised the crowd as members from our stake.

"We're almost here," I whispered to Bridget triumphantly. Tears ran down Mum's cheek as she saw the end in sight. I saw the youths' faces light up with beams of happiness as they saw their families waiting for them. I really enjoyed watching everyone's happy expressions as we neared the end. While Dad, Mum and I didn't have any family to greet us over the finish line, I had now learnt to see my fellow church members as my family. For the first time I felt accepted in the church and that I belonged there. It was an amazing feeling to see all my fellow members waiting and cheering, and I felt as if they were cheering just for me. I felt the same sense of unity with them as I had just felt singing with the youth.

Dad reached over and hugged me once we had crossed the line. "I'm so proud of you and everything that you have achieved," Dad told me. "And I'm not just talking about trek," he added. "I'm talking about all the changes that you've made in your life. You've come such a long way."

"Thanks, Dad," I replied, returning his hug. "We all have."

I always had trouble relating to pioneers, but now, for the first time, I felt as if their story was a part of me. I knew that what I had been through could not compare in any way to what they had been through. Nor could I even begin to understand what they had suffered for the gospel's sake. But I did now recognise what their journey had been all about, and I felt a common purpose with them. The reasons for our journeys were the same. We were inspired by our love for God and our desire to follow our Saviour Jesus Christ. We were all putting our lives on the altar, just in different ways. It was this understanding that made trek such a profound experience for me.

I contentedly took another look at the clapping and cheering crowd, and I couldn't believe who I saw. Standing at the back of the crowd was our godfather. He stood with Paul and his other followers, and he was clapping as proudly as any other member of the stake. The godfather smiled at me when he saw me look in his direction and gave me a wink. He had always been so stern, so aloof, so intimidating whenever I had met him in the past. I was shocked to see him acting so warmly, almost affectionately.

Bridget and Carly's parents rushed over to them and gave them each a big embrace. Bridget returned her parents' embrace warmly. Carly looked embarrassed as her mother threw her arms around her but looked pleased all the same. Yes, it was good to be home, I thought. Peter turned my way as he saw his parents and five siblings pushing their way through the crowd towards him. I affectionately threw my arms around Peter, and Peter just held me in his arms for a moment. "Thanks for everything, Peter," I told him. Peter smiled kindly at me and gave me a final goodbye wave before walking towards his family. I again looked over at our godfather. I was still amazed that he was here, celebrating our completion of trek with us. The godfather cast a final smile in my direction before turning and striding away through the late afternoon sun, the others following him. I never saw the godfather again. That life was no longer a part of my life. I was now a pioneer.

ABOUT THE AUTHOR

Sean Kikkert was born in Adelaide, South Australia. He spent the early part of his childhood in the Netherlands, where his father worked as a scientist, before returning to Australia. As a fifteen year old, he was given a copy of the Book of Mormon by an elder brother. This sacred text powerfully built on the foundation of faith formed by the example of his deeply religious mother. Though he had to wait till he was a bit older before he could be baptised, he considered himself a convert to The Church of Jesus Christ of Latter-day Saints before his first visit to a church meeting or his first lesson with the missionaries.

Sean served in the Australia Sydney South Mission. He then earnt a honors bachelor's degree before completing a law degree with honors at the University of Adelaide. He married his wife Elizabeth in the Sydney Australia Temple, and they are the parents of five children.

Sean's first job after becoming a lawyer brought him and his family to Canberra, Australia's capital city, and to the very same ward where he had started his mission. He has served as a bishopric counsellor, bishop and stake young men president. He currently serves as the gospel doctrine teacher in his ward.